Amrapalli and Other Stories

Amrapalli and Other Stories

Surendra Mohanty

Translated from Odia by

Sambit Panigrahi

BLACK EAGLE BOOKS
Dublin, USA | Bhubaneswar, India

Black Eagle Books
USA address:
7464 Wisdom Lane
Dublin, OH 43016

India address:
E/312, Trident Galaxy, Kalinga Nagar,
Bhubaneswar-751003, Odisha, India

E-mail: info@blackeaglebooks.org
Website: www.blackeaglebooks.org

First International Edition Published by
Black Eagle Books, 2023

AMRAPALLI AND OTHER STORIES
by **Surendra Mohanty**

Translated from Odia by **Sambit Panigrahi**

Cover & Interior Design: Ezy's Publication

ISBN- 978-1-64560-434-1 (Paperback)
Library of Congress Control Number: 2023944594

Printed in the United States of America

CONTENT

Translator's Note

A celebrated Odia writer, Surendra Mohanty was born on 21 June 1922 and he passed away on 21 December 1990. Mohanty has been a writer possessing a remarkable creative prowess, and he penned numerous fictional and non-fictional works that have continued to remain insignias of his undying contribution to the vast literary reservoir of Odia language and culture. Besides being a writer of unique distinction, Mohanty also occupied many important literary and political positions in the state of Odisha. He worked as the president of Odisha Sahitya Academy from 1981 to 1987 and he was also the first editor, and later chief editor for the famous Odia newspaper *The Sambad*. The literary and critical outputs of Surendra Mohanty are immense and variegated; his writings encompass a wide variety of genres and categories; he is a writer of short stories, novels, travelogues, criticism and biographies. Mohanty wrote around 50 books belonging to different genres encompassing literary and non-literary productions. Some of his well-known novels are *Nilasaila* (*The Blue Mountain*) and *Andha Diganta* (*The Dark Horizon*). *Mahanirvana* (*The Salvation*), *Yadubansa* (The Yadu Dynasty), *Mahanagarira Ratri* (*Night in the City*), *Rajadhani* (The Capital City), *Krushnachuda* (The

Gulmohur) and *Ruti O Chandra* (Bread and The Moon) etc. are some of his famous short stories.

Apart from being a litterateur of great eminence, Mohanty was also a renowned politician and a member of parliament in 1957.

Translating Surendra Mohanty is a unique experience for various reasons. Many literary critics have unanimously agreed that Surendra Mohanty is at his creative best when he pens down his short stories. The most admirable qualities that his short stories possess is that they are not restricted to any particular theme or area; rather, they encompass an extensive variety of subject matters including history, mythology, modernity, the evolving society and the changing individual etc. The varied spectrum of themes, areas and concerns that he introduces in his stories provide him wide recognition, fame and acceptability as a writer amongst the audience. Mohanty seems to have developed a particular interest in Buddhism and its history for which he has penned some of his stories like "Pita Putra" ("Father and Son") and "Mahanirvana" ("The Salvation") and in my estimation, some of Mohanty's finest stories are in fact his stories based on Buddhism and its history.

It is worth mentioning at this juncture that Mohanty also takes special interest in depicting fragmented episodes of Indian mythology whose biggest testimony is his story "Srikrushnanka Sesha Hasa" (Srikrishna's Last Laugh) where he borrows an important and fascinating episode from *The Mahabharata* and presents it before the audience in the form of an elaborated story. By penning down such mythological stories, Mohanty not only showcases another specimen of his phenomenal artistry as a creative artist, but also acquaints the readers with such forgotten or less known but defining episodes of the great Indian epics like *The Mahabharata.*

Apart from mythological stories, Mohanty also focuses on realistic stories the subject matters of which have emanated from his the felt, real life experiences of diverse sections of people representing different milieus and generations from the pre-independent to the post-independent times. For instance, his story "Dinosar-ra Atma" ("The Soul of the Dinosaur") is exclusively based on the lost, forlorn glory and grandeur of kingship in the post-independent era where a previous king, bereft of the power and authority of royalty, finds himself like a dinosaur—a rare specimen of an extinct species.

Some of Mohanty's stories are also intensely political in nature where he covertly expresses his political views and ideologies through his characters who embody different political ideologies and predilections. One such story is "Ruti O Chandra" ("Bread and Moon") where Mohanty offers intense criticism of Marxism by exposing its stark indifference to delicate human feelings and sentiments and its over-indulgence in economic indicators as the only determinants of human lives and human values.

In the midst of Mohanty's multifaceted literary craftsmanship, one cannot however undermine the fact that one of his finest narrative crafts is humour which he particularly employs in some of his stories on politics and academia. It goes without saying that Mohanty's humour originates from his minute observations of the undercurrent of blatant hypocrisy existing in the realm of politics and of the falsely sophisticated and propagandist nature of our academia. Some such stories that exemplify Mohanty's remarkable humour-generating literary craftsmanship are

"Rajadhani" ("The Capital") and "Vagabond" etc. where he comically exposes and gleefully ridicules some of our follies and hypocrisies that we hide under the garb of cultural and intellectual sophistication.

After this brief introduction on some of the predominant themes of Mohanty's stories, I must now share with the audience some of my own experiences of translating Mohanty from Odia to English. It is famously said by eminent American poet Robert Frost that "Poetry is what is lost in translation"—a statement that indicates the impossibility, on the translator's part, of the total transfer of the original text's whole essence into the translated text. It must be understood that each language is embedded with cultural values and nuances specific to its own and these culture-specific ethos and practices are perhaps linguistically untranslatable. Certain typical Odia-language-specific colloquial expressions, which Mohanty is adept in frequently using in his writing, are perhaps the best instances of the much-talked about case of cultural untranslatability. As a translator of Mohanty's short stories, I have tried my level best to negotiate between two languages and two cultures that are supposedly diametrically opposite to each other so far as their respective norms, ethos and praxes are concerned. It must be comprehended nevertheless that absolute fidelity to the original text both in terms total and undistorted transference of textual meaning and cultural significations is an absolute impossibility.

It must also be pointed out at this juncture that Mohanty, in spite of his illustrious stature as a celebrated Odia writer, can however be accused of occasional indulgence in unwarranted verbosity in his writing. Of course, it is also understood that a writer's creativity has limitless dimensions and he cannot be bound by any specific dictum or formula so far as his narrative, stylistic and linguistic experimentations are concerned. However, over-abundance of terseness, verbosity and colloquation in writing might offer bitter challenges for the translator and perhaps, it happens to be the case, occasionally though, during the translation of Mohanty's works. Of course, translating verbose sentences and expressions might look a bit difficult and challenging; however, it can also not be denied that reproducing the same sentences with utmost clarity and simplicity in the target language text is an immensely pleasurable and enlightening experience.

At the end, I thank my family members including my parents and wife who stood by me all through my effort. And at last my prayer to Lord Jagannath.

Sambit Panigrahi

Translation: Problems, Possibilities and Strategies

Defining Translation

Translation is an act of creating a bridge between different languages and cultures and the process involves multiples skills and strategies adopted by the translator at semantic, linguistic and cultural levels. The act of translation involves no abstraction, but an intensely engaging practice that tends towards achieving perfection through the continually improving grasp and comprehension of two languages and two cultures on the translator's part. The act of translation, according to many critics, is also a creative activity which makes a work survive the constraints of time and space and transcend the boundaries of specific languages and cultures and thereby attain space-less and timeless universality. Translation thus becomes an inter-cultural and inter-linguistic mediator and an upholder of the work's aesthetic permanence, cutting across regions, cultures and languages along with specific, geographical, national and other spatio-temporal demarcations. The value and significance of translation is immense, particularly in a continually proliferating cosmopolitan scenario where intercultural and inter-linguistic permeability is equally essential and rampant.

It must be comprehended that language is an integral part of culture and they can never be seen in absolute isolation. Therefore, an act of translation not only involves a process of semantic transference of meaning from the source-language-text to the target-language-text, but also a concomitant process of transference of cultural ethos and values. Snell-Hornby rightly puts it as:

> The concept of culture as a totality of knowledge, proficiency and perception is fundamental in our approach to translation. If language is an integral part of culture, the translator needs not only proficiency in two languages, he must also be at home in two cultures. In other words, he must be bilingual and bicultural. (Snell-Hornby 2001: 42)

In this context, translation can be regarded as an assimilative process that offers "a means of studying cultural interaction" (Lefevere and Bassnett 2001: 6), and in this scenario, a translator can be seen as a communicative mediator between cultures which may even be diametrically opposite to each other. In other words, it means that the translator can manipulate differences between languages and cultures in a way that he can come up with a new product that carries emblems of multicultural ethos, values and nuances. In this process, the translator establishes a sense of linguistic and cultural hybridity and reinforces the notion propounded by Edward Said that in our age, "all cultures are involved in one another; none is single and pure, all are hybrid, heterogeneous, extraordinarily differentiated, and unmonolithic."

From another perspective, translation can be seen as an act of liberation; it emancipates the text from the incarcerations of one, particular cultural and linguistic signifying system in the sense that the text no more remains subordinate to the constricting domain of the source language and culture. In this process of the liberating the text from one cultural-linguistic barrier, translation endeavours to bridge the abyssal gap between the source-language-text and the target-language-text. Such an act entails an essential process of creativity so much so that the act of translation remains essentially a never-ending dialogic process between languages and their attendant cultures.

The Status of Translation as a Secondary Product

One also has to grapple with the perennial critical problem of translation being always ascribed with a secondary status and the translated product being considered as a secondary product as compared to the original work. This discrimination has continued for quite a long time and has created some kind of a binary between the original work and the translated product where the former is considered superior and the latter inferior. This discrimination has perpetually vexed the critical minds and a probable solution is provided with the advent of poststructuralism in the realm of critical thinking, particularly under the aegis of Derrida's introduction of the notion of 'deconstruction' — a notion that dismantles all binaries: high art/low art, mainstream literature/secondary literature etc.

The instauration of this radical and innovative perception in the domain of critical thinking paves the way for a possible solution to this problem of inherent discrimination between two forms of literary products and such discriminations start being considered arbitrary, constructed and superfluous. Thus, poststructural thought creates a situation where both the original work and the translated product are measured with an equal status and dignity.

In this situation, Indian thought and philosophy have helped a great deal to deconstruct this pre-existing binary—a scenario that has been thoroughly explored by eminent linguist G. N. Devy who, in his remarkable essay "Literary History and Translation," has exclusively dealt with the issue of discrimination between two forms of literature. According to Devy, it is the western philosophy that has historically premised itself on the binary of the self/other (which is the source, originator and mother of all other subsequent binaries) whereas in Indian philosophy, this self/other distinction does not exist at all as we are all conceived as mere reflections of the 'purusha' which is the ultimate truth and the creator of all. In this context, Sudhir Kakkar alludes to *Katha Upanaishada* which elucidates this concept of 'purusha' in emphatic terms:

> The tree of eternity has its roots in heaven above and its branches reach down to earth. It is Brahman. . . Beyond the senses is the spirit of man, and beyond this is the spirit of the universe, and evolver of all. And beyond is Purusha, all pervading, beyond definitions.

In this situation, when we are all mere reflections of a bigger truth that is one, unique and all-pervasive, then no body is a 'self' and nobody is an 'other' and everybody is a shadow, a mere reflection of one, bigger, all-encompassing, universal entity. In such a situation, there is no question of conceiving entities through binaries and such binaries are considered presumptuously arbitrary, unfounded and artificial. In addition, Devy highlights Sudhir Kakkar's distinction between two other Indian philosophical concets—'vidya' and 'avidya'— by saying that 'vidya' is true knowledge that spreads from the 'soul' to the 'self' whereas 'avidya' is false knowledge that spreads from the 'self' to the 'soul' and thus, the distinction between 'self' and 'other,' in Indian theological epistemology, is invalid and such a distinction is considered to be 'avidya' or 'maya.' On the other hand, the western episteme is predominantly premised on this 'self/other' distinction whereas this distinction in the realm of the Indian episteme is redundant, illusory and is tantamount to becoming nothing but 'maya' and 'avidya.' This is the fundamental difference between Indian and western epistemologies. Sudhir Kakkar states:

> The distinction between 'vidya' and 'avidya'—true and false consciousness—between 'reality' and 'maya,' illustrate a fundamental difference between Hindu and Western world images. . . The maintenance of ego-boundaries, between inside and outside, and between I and others is the staff of reality in Western thought, yet Maya to the Hindus.

Following this line of argument, one can deduce the inference that in the Indian context, the distinction between the 'self' and the 'other' and its analogic distinction between the mainstream literature and translation is tantamount to the spread of false knowledge or 'avidya' and 'maya.'

In other words, translation has historically held the same relevance and importance as does mainstream literature. Moreover, Devy also states that the Indian subcontinent, unlike the west, has a very rich and profound tradition of multiculturalism and multilingualism where multiple cultures and multiples languages are accepted and celebrated in the Indian literary firmament where no difference or distinction between them is entertained. In India, Writers of Greek ancestry Asvaghosha, of Irish nationality Nivedita, and of Arabian training Ibn Battuta have been accepted as Indian writers. Moreover, some of the great classics in India have originated from acts of translation; *Jnaneswari* in Marathi, Kamban's *Ramayana* in Kannada, Tulsi Das' *Ramayana* in Hindi etc. are some of its prime examples. In addition, India has also a very strong bilingual tradition. When Panini wrote his grammar in pre-Christian centuries, he spoke of two discourses in Sanskrit, one used by the common populace and another that is grammatically correct. When Bharata theorized dramatic conventions in *Natyasastra*, he spoke of two types of theatre, one catering to the public and the other, based on rigid, dramatic conventions. In 11th Century, Rakasekhara could write plays both in Sanskrit & Maharastri. In 12th Century, Jayadeva wrote poetry in Sanskrit & Bengali. In 13th Century, Hemachandra wrote in Sanskrit and Gujurati. Namadeva wrote poetry in Hindi, Punjabi, Marathi. In addition, we have many Indian writers who write in many languages simultaneously—in Hindi & Urdu, in Odia and Bangla, in Odia and English, in English and Bangla etc. These examples of bilingual or multilingual textual productions in India at different points in time attest to the fact that India has a very strong tradition of translation cutting across languages and cultures and it is through this act of translation, texts belonging to particular languages and cultures have achieved pan-Indian acceptability.

Translation or Transcreation?

Now in the general context of the discussion on theorizing translation, one must also confront the question of fidelity in translation, that is to say, whether an act of translation should maintain absolute faithfulness to the original author and his work or whether he can exercise certain amount of creative liberty during the act of translation. In this regard, one can trace a chronological evolution of different ideas and understandings starting from the older to the present times. For instance, during the era of Biblical translation, absolute fidelity to the original text was the inviolable norm or principle and no liberty of any kind whatsoever was granted for the translator. But with the progress of time, both the translator and the critical audience observed and realized the unnaturalness, incongruities and anomalies that popped up during these kinds of translations that were exclusively premised on the notions of absolute fidelity and faithfulness to the 'original.' And also, with the development of the notions like "Death of the Author" by Roland Barthes and "What is an Author" by Michel Foucault along with the phenomenal rise of the post-structuralist realm of thought, pioneered by Derrida and his followers, the longstanding and preconceived notion of the author's originality was seriously problematized. The author was readily displaced from his previously uncontested position of being the sole originator of his work and no work could now be considered as 'original' in the strict and conventional sense of the term. Now, one starts asking the pertinent question that if the author cannot claim originality to his work, then where lies the question of absolute fidelity to the original work during an act of translation?

Thus in this new scenario, a simplistic word-to-word or sentence-to-sentence rendering is a mere impossibility, neither it is desired or advocated. The translator's constructive intervention and innovation both at thematic and linguistic levels make the act of translation more effective and fruitful and the translated product widely acceptable in the target language culture while a mere word-to-word translation makes the translated work linguistically and culturally untenable. Trying to achieve exact equivalence between the Source Language Text (SLT) and the Target Language Text (TLT), however, was practiced and promoted at the early stages of translation and absolute rigidity was maintained while no scope for creative innovation was entertained at all. But since no two languages and two cultures bear exact equivalence and since each language is culture- specific and is different from the other language that has its own typical cultural specificities, such an act of translation striving for exact equivalence leads towards the translated work becoming more incongruous, unpalatable and unnatural. And curtailing the translator's liberty and incarcerating him with the binding principle of exact equivalence proves to be disastrous and leads towards the untoward creation of linguistic and cultural anomalies. The translator's confined role as a mere renderer of linguistic equivalence and as a mere conveyer of meaning has progressively become a topic for debate, discussion and interrogation from the critics. With the progress of time, an urgency is felt to attribute more autonomy to the translator so that he could assume the role of some kind of a creator in a scenario where the act of translation tends towards becoming a creative act rather than becoming a mere simplistic, superficial and mechanical meaning-conveying exercise. In such an altered scenario, translation tends towards becoming transcreation. The lately developed theories of poststructuralism facilitate the process enormously by highlighting the polysemous nature of language and its nonconformity to a single, monolithic pattern of meaning. The inherently slippery nature of language is understood and its productive capability for a wide and extensive array of significations is thoroughly realized—a realization that ultimately liberates both the translator and his act of translation from the clutches of mere linguistic conveyance of meaning and signification.

This is why in today's parlance, a work of translation tends towards becoming a work of transcreation (a term coined by Indian poet/translator/editor from Calcutta P. Lal) where the translator can afford to exercise his creative liberty to produce a work that, despite its conventional and supposed allegiance to the original work, can take the shape of what eminent translation critic Sujit Mukherjee would call 'new writing.' Mukherjee interestingly cites the usual acronyms of the word 'translation' in the Indian context which are 'rupantar' (changed in form) and 'anuvad' ('speaking after' or 'following after') and as the meanings of these acronyms suggest, neither of them implicates and advocates absolute equivalence in meaning. It means that the traditional understanding of the concept of translation in the Indian context never premises itself around the notion of absolute fidelity or faithfulness to the original. In his interesting essay "Translation as New Writing," Sujit Mukherjee beautifully elucidates how translation in our part of the world (in an interesting contradiction to the West) has historically evolved as 'new writing' where the translator has always enjoyed the liberty to exercise his own creative freedom during his act of translation. While citing multiple instances of the translation of great Indian epics by various regional translators, Mukherjee shows how these translators have, in their own significant ways, recreated the original Sanskrit epics like *The Mahabharata* and *The Ramayana* in their respective vernaculars. Pampa's *Pampabharata* in Kannada is, in fact, a new rendering of the original Sanskrit Mahabharata. This is precisely why the new translators preferred to call him Abhinava Pampa so that he could be differentiated, at symbolic and metaphoric levels, from the original Papma; so also is the case of Abhinava Vyasa. In a similar vein, Bengali poet Alol's Bengali version of Malik Muhammad Jayasi's 15th Century Hindi work *Pudmavat* is almost a new writing. These vernacular versions of the mentioned great Indian epics can no more be considered works of mere translation; rather, they are new writings that have been able to generate specific identities of their own as distinctive and independent literary productions that can exist on their own, irrespective of their essential indebtedness to their original Sanskrit versions.

In this context, I view my own work of translation not merely as a work of translation, but rather, as a work of transcreation, as a 'new writing,' which while sufficiently acknowledging its indebtedness to the original work in Odia, also adequately claims for its own novelty, independence and self-sufficiency. In the context of translation being 'new writing,' one can read A. K. Ramanujan's essay "Three Hundred *Ramayanas*" (though Ramanujan has not used the term 'new writing') where he shows that there are multiple versions of *Ramayana*s existing in the northern and southern parts of India. In one version, Ravana is a highly educated ascetic Brahmin; in another version, Sita happens to be Ravana's daughter whereas in another version, Laxmana and not Rama slays Ravana. So, the epic *Ramayana* existing in multiple forms and varieties in India and outside, are palimpsests of new writings rather than being mere translations of the original Sanskrit *Ramayana* by Valmiki. This leads to a comprehension that translation is extremely important for the wider acceptability of a literary text through its multiple forms, variations and manifestations cutting across regions, generations, cultures and languages in a scenario where translation indulges not merely in rendering meanings, but rather in creating new significations. This, in turn, demystifies the presumed differences between creative writing and translation in a scenario where translation is equally a creative endeavour as is the original one.

The Question of Untranslatability

It was Robert Frost who once opined that 'poetry is what is lost in translation'—a statement that is overtly implicative of the fact that an act of translation perennially involves a process of loss of meaning. Though an eminent litterateur like Frost spoke only about the loss during the act of translation, there could also be gain during the same, which he willy-nilly overlooked. So, the process of translation involves both loss and gain (of meaning) at various levels— linguistic, cultural, semantic and epistemological. However, in the 1950s, "postformalist" Roman Jacobson disparaged the concept of untranslatability that "everything and nothing" is translatable, and claimed that untranslatability is no more than mere dogma. According to Jacobson, great modernists like James Joyce and Ezra Pound, have elucidated to us that the situation of "untranslatability" is indeed an opportunity for creative inventions, for making it new. Current translation scholars like Lawrence Venuti, a translator of Italian literature, emphasize that translation as creative interpretation is the ultimate humanistic task, not only because it keeps literary works alive, but because it is an interpretive act that attributes an immense variety to the form, meaning and effect of the source text.

Thus, it is the job of the translator to be an effective negotiator between the questions of loss and the gain during the act of translation and he has to make a delicate balance between the two perennial problematics of translation. It is the translator's onus to create a product that is the fruitful negotiator between two languages and two cultures such that he is able to generate a never-ending dialogue between two languages and cultures that had so far remained aloof and alienated. Through translation, different languages and cultures enter into a complex dialogic forum where there are constant linguistic and cultural confrontations, exchanges, mediations, negotiations, semantic and epistemological transferences, superimpositions, replacements, substitutions and recuperations.

The translator can confront and grapple with the question of untranslatability by devising multiple techniques and strategies such that certain untranslatable words and expressions can be reproduced in the Target-Language-Text in a more comprehensible manner. In this situation, the translator has to devise effective means and strategies to negotiate with this eternal problem, i.e., the question of untranslatability. He could provide notes, glossaries and other explanations to convey the meaning of the untranslatable words or expressions that are colloquial and exclusively culture-specific. We come across many such situations where translators are found to be using such means and strategies to effectively negotiate this problem and provide pertinent solution to this perennial problem of untranslatability in a way that the translated product attains a significant degree of innovativeness and creativity.

Types of Translation: The Underlying Power-Dynamics

Now let's turn our attention to two major and different kinds of translation—exotropic translation and endotropic translation. Exotropic translation is a kind of translation where an indigenous language is translated into a foreign language while endotropic translation is one where just the reverse happens, i.e., a foreign language is translated into an indigenous language. However, it must be understood that both processes involve different kinds of politics and power-dynamics at linguistic and cultural levels where one language endeavours to superimpose its cultural patterns over the other and vice versa. As Anuradha Dingwaney puts it: "The processes of translation involved in making another culture comprehensible entail varying degrees of violence, especially when the culture being translated is constituted as that of the "other." No act of translation is culturally, linguistically and politically neutral and in every such act, there is the involvement of clandestine cultural and political warfare reinforced by several cultural/linguistic forces of acceptance, resistance, tensions and of negotiations etc.

So, there is no denying of the fact that every act of translation involves itself with an extremely complex and two- way process of cultural and linguistic cold-war. Robert J. C. Young in his essay "Postcolonialism: A Very Short Introduction to Translation" makes interesting observations of how during the colonial times, translation was used as an effective tool by the colonizers to superimpose their cultural values and patterns on the indigenous culture by promoting translation of indigenous texts into the colonizer's language, such as English. In such a strategy, they not only imposed their language on the language of the colonized, but also domesticated the original vernacular texts by getting them translated into English. In this process, the indigenous language and culture started getting dominated and in a way, they started losing their indigenous relevance with the progress of time with significant damage done to their ethos and nuances. This situation was gravely escalated by rampant cases exotropic translations promoted by the colonizers. However, with 'decolonization' setting in, dissenting voices arose from within the colonized landscape and concerted efforts were made to reassert the immense literary worth of the indigenous literature. The tremendous body of indigenous literature now becomes exposed to the closed colonial minds and the literary horizon of the indigenous literature is significantly expanded and globalized through such acts of translation.

But it is also pertinent to establish here that 'decolonization' has done tremendous good to the exposition of indigenous literature and culture by reinforcing their undeniable impact on colonial language and literature, even in case of exotropic translation. Certain indigenous words, colloquial expressions etc. have made inroads into the language of the colonizer and the colonizer is made to accept such linguistic and cultural encroachments into his linguistic/cultural domain. In this process, the colonizer's self-assumed linguistic and cultural superiority gets significantly dismantled. In an era of continually proliferating linguistic and cultural permeability, one can also aim to dismantle the difference between exotropic and endotropic translation and both translations can be advocated and promoted in equal measures.

Strategies of Translation

Eminent translation theorist Lawrence Venuti, in his famous essay "The Cultural Politics of Translation," discusses two major strategies of translation—domestication and foreignization. The domestication strategy of translation is a strategy that believes in the appropriation of the linguistic and cultural phenomena of the Source Language Text (SLT) into that of the Target Language Text (TLT). In other words, in this kind of translation, the linguistic and cultural patterns, ethos and peculiarities of the (SLT) are domesticated inside the cultural domain of the (TLT) such that the whole corpus of the (SLT) along with its cultural underpinnings, its linguistic, syntactic and semantic nuances and peculiarities are all assimilated or rather, domesticated into the culture of the TLT. This kind of translation was heavily practiced from 16th Century onwards up to 19th Century in the realm of translation activities; however, this kind of domestication strategy always continued to remain problematic for its negligence, overlook and obliteration of the nuanced cultural patterns of the SLT which, in a way, facilitated the unquestionable supremacy of the TLT's linguistic and cultural all-pervasiveness.

Compared to the domesticating strategies of translation, however, the foreignizing strategy of translation makes the reader realize that the source language and culture have their nuances, peculiarities and specificities that are to be preserved and represented by the

TLT in a way that the linguistic, semantic, epistemological and cultural differences between the SLT and TLT are respected, maintained and preserved. In this process, the reader becomes positively and critically aware of the inherent peculiarities of each language and its associated culture. Through foreignizing strategy, the TLT and its associated culture gravitate towards the SLT and its associated culture in a way that the falsely presumptive cultural ascendancy of the TLT over the SLT is undermined and obliterated. Through the foreignizing strategy, each of the two languages is able to maintain its cultural dignity, and the two yet are brought closer to each other through the dialogic and interactive process of translation. And in this process, the inevitable ethnic violence that happens in an act of translation is significantly minimized.

So far as my particular act of translation is concerned, I have adopted the foreignizing strategy and my translation is a classic case of exotrpoic translation. Through this foreignizing strategy, my translation resists the domestication of the source language, i.e. Odia by the target language culture, i.e. English and the specific identity of the Odia language and culture is thoroughly preserved. I can cite certain examples where there certain Odia words which are either untranslatable or they do not possess exact equivalence in the English language or culture; in this situation, I have retained these Odia words and have provided footnotes that explain these words or colloquial expressions in English such that the English reader gets a sense of what these words or expressions may refer to. In this way, the Odia cultural nuances and specificities are preserved whereas their implications are explained in English such that they do not get totally missed out or obliterated from the TLT. This is a classic case of foreignizing strategy where the Odia language with its attendant cultural ethos is represented in English, yet, it is not domesticated in the English language. Such typical cases also, apart from resisting domestication, dismantle the domination/subjugation binary that previously existed between languages, artificially though.

Conclusion

There are varying degrees of understanding amongst critical readers regarding the role and significance of the translator and the act of translation. One group of critics do adopt a universalist, humanist approach towards the act of translation as an activity that bridges cultural gaps and generates an amicable sense of literary homogeneity across languages and cultures whereas another group of critics do evaluate an act of translation much more critically, with an intent in discovering the clandestine politics, violence and strategies involved in an act of translation. According to these critics, translation is an intensely political act that is both a corroborator and perpetuator of social, linguistic and cultural hierarchies and hegemonies amongst different cultural and linguistic communities. As Susan Bassanet explains:

According to one reading of the translator's role, the translator is a force for good, a creative artist who ensures the survival of writing across time and space, an intercultural mediator and interpreter, a figure whose importance to the continuity and diffusion of culture is immeasurable. In contrast, another interpretation sees translation as a highly suspect activity, one in which an inequality of power relations (inequalities of economics, politics, gender and geography) is reflected in the mechanics of textual production. (4)

However, one must comprehend that in spite of the immense diversity of critical understandings and approaches towards translation, all critical thinkers do emphasize on the socio-cultural backdrop against which the textual productions occur during an act of translation. There is absolutely no denying of the fact that 'translation studies' has evolved as a huge and relentlessly evolving literary and critical industry and has established itself as an epicentre of the tremendously escalating scholarly attentions around this novel area of study.

It must be also emphasized here that the non-European and particularly, the oriental world's approach towards translation has been much more progressive, unorthodox and liberational compared to the usually rigid, orthodox and limitational view of translation upheld by the western literary canon for so long—a point well-taken by the eminent translation theorist Susan Bassanet in her foundational book on translation theory, *Translation Studies*. The orientalist translation scholars and critics have always estimated a work of translation as a creative engagement with the original work on the part of the translator or in other words, they have always viewed the work of translation as a creative process instead of being a mere imitational mirror-image reflection of the original work. In the worldview inculcated in this part of the world, the translator is perceived as an emancipator who liberates the text from the incarcerations of socio-linguistic codes, conventions and bondages of the original language and culture thereby making it accessible and amenable to another language and culture. Such a progressive and liberational comprehension of the act of translation also is involved in an acknowledgement, promotion and pronouncement of the inherent acumen of creativity involved in the act of translation. This kind of progressive, liberative and assimilative approach can be said to be essentially dialogic in nature (to use a typical Bakhtinian terminology) where two languages and two cultures are in constant dialogue with each other in a scenario where no language or culture achieves supremacy or ascendancy over the other and vice versa. I would claim in this context that my approach in this translation is essentially a dialogic approach since I do not see any hierarchical difference between my source language Odia (my mother tongue) and the target language English into which I have translated the short stories of Surendra Mohanty.

In this context, we can argue that an act of translation does not merely generate a word-to-word correspondence between the SLT and TLT, rather generates the possibility of multiple significations—a notion that can be metaphorically enunciated by famous translation theorist Andre Lefebvre's conceptualization of translation being a refraction rather than a reflection of the original. A mere reflection will create a replica of the original with a linear and singular signification whereas a refraction will create the same replica, but with multiple significations and interpretative possibilities. Texts, according to Lefebvre, are inevitable products of complex, signifying systems and the translator's unique endeavour is to decode and re-encode these components.

Another important view that has developed about translation is that it genuinely attributes an 'after-life' to the text which attains a new 'originality' in the target language and culture. Translation presents itself as a trans-spatial and trans-temporal activity; it acts as a dialogic forum for inter-spatial, inter-cultural and inter-temporal negotiations. The text, which otherwise would have become obsolete or forgotten in the source language, achieves artistic and aesthetic permanence when translated to other languages through which it survives the taste of time and age. Susan Bassanet provides Josephine Balmer's excellent example of how less-known women poets of ancient Greece have survived the onslaught of time and are remembered only through translation. So, translation's positive role in making the text survive through time is unquestionable. In this particular case of translation of Surendra Mohanty's Odia stories into English, there is no denying of the fact that it is only through the act of translation that a writer like Surendra Mohanty who would otherwise have been confined to the domains of Odia language and culture, can be read and remembered in other languages, in English, for instance, in this particular context.

In the context of this overall discussion on translation, one must examine the presence or voice of the translator in the text vis-à-vis the presence or the voice of the original author which is overt, proclamatory and self-sufficient. But on the other hand, the translator's voice can have various manifestations; it can be overt, or covert, vociferous or camouflaged and thus, can have various manifestations relating to the multiple cultural and ideological crosscurrents that have collectively produced him/her. Theo Hermans, in his interesting essay "The Translator's Voice in Translated Narrative," takes up this issue of the translator's voice which he considers as the "index of the translator's discursive presence" (27). According to Hermans, the voice may remain concealed behind that of the author, thus making itself invisible or unheard. Or else, he may have a vehement and voluble presence through a paratextual 'Translator's Note' thereby manifesting as an auto-referential first person having thorough identification with the original narrative voice.

If one casts a cursory glance and the history and at the progressive evolution of the process of translation, he/she shall find that at the initial stages (during the early stages of biblical translation, for instance), the translator's voice was forced into self-effacement only to make the original writer's voice lone, prominent and sui generis whereas the translator's position was evaluated as being a passive and inaudible renderer of a second order of signifying system. But with the progress of time and with the growing comprehension of the nuanced and clandestine, socio-political and ideological cross-currents that regulate the act of translation, the translator is now being considered as a "co-producer of the discourse" (Hermans 42). Theo Hermans envisages the role, presence and voice of the translator not as a static, sedentary and passive renderer or transporter of meaning and signification, but as a dialogic negotiator between distinctive and previously non-interactive and non-mutual domains of textual formations and semantic and epistemological significations. Hermans explains beautifully: "The model, that is, needs to incorporate the Translator as constantly co-producing the discourse, shadowing, mimicking and, as it were, counterfeiting the Narrator's words, but occasionally — caught in the text's disparities and interstices; and paratextually — emerging into the open as a separate discursive presence" (43).

Amrapalli

I

That day, the conference hall of Baisali's Lichhabbi'[1]-union could not spare some space even for a piece of grain. It was jam-packed. Everybody, starting from the commoners, the royal personages, the intellectuals, and the businessmen, had assembled there to witness the assembly's proceedings and to listen to the union's ultimate judgement on Amrapalli[2].

In such gatherings on other occasions, one hardly found the simultaneous presence of all the members of the commoners' union inside the gigantic hall's vast and expansive inner space; but today, all had occupied their respective positions inside the hall with utmost excitement and enthusiasm; they waited for the instructions of the convener to commence the proceedings.

---

1   It's a clan that lived in the ancient Indian kingdom of Magadha.
2   Amrapalli was a beautiful lady of Magadha during 500 BC (roughly) who had to turn into a public whore under certain circumstances as described in the story. She ultimately became Lord Buddha's disciple.

The convener sprung from his seat to pacify the noisy and bustling audience and stated: "Please listen to me, respected members. There is no urgency for maintaining quorum today. Because, as far as I can observe, almost all the members of the Licchabbi community are present here, in this grave and auspicious occasion. Therefore, I humbly request the chief whip to commence the proceedings." At the instructions of the convener, the chief whip Deepankara stood up from his seat and stated while addressing the audience, emphatically: "Esteemed convener and all the respected members of the committee. May I kindly have your attention, please? Before listening to the committee's final judgement on Amrapalli, please listen to her life story narrated by her foster-father, the gardener Asitabarna."

Asitabarna stood up from amidst the swarming assemblage of the commoners, stared at the amassed crowd with a hawk-eyed, revolving glare, paid soulful obeisance to them with folded hands and said: "Dear commoners! I am the mango orchard's caretaker at Baisali's[3] outskirts. Today, I recapitulate my life's most preposterous yet memorable event that occurred sixteen years ago, inside this mango orchard. The orchard was filled with a dense foliage of trees and with the flooding moonlight of the radiant moon that had soared high up into the sky like a golden-winged eagle. It was not yet morning. The collective, restless twitters of the morning-birds woke me up from bed, very early, when the reddish sun was just beginning to bloom like a lone, incandescent lotus in the eastern sky. The wind had gotten heavier with the fragrance of the proliferating mango buds inside the orchard, and their intoxicating smell initiated me into the slow, savoury advent of the blooming dawn.

---

3   An ancient Indian city.

I suddenly heard the relentless cry of a new-born baby lying abandoned in a secluded corner's chequered gloom inside the orchard. I had been childless all my life and had always longed for one. I wondered whether it was a crude game of destiny or God almighty's providence lying strewn before me as a rare and prodigious gift. I remember that day vividly even today, despite the old-age-induced impairment of my memory and with all my past reminiscences having slipped irretrievably into oblivion. That day, some destitute lady had abandoned this beautiful baby below a mango tree; even her umbilical cord was not severed. Without contemplating anything, I lifted her onto my lap. I did not bother whether she was an obnoxious whore's blasphemous child or even a curse to mankind; I readily accepted her as my own child. Sixteen years later, today she is your Amrapalli—Baisali's ill-fated beauty."

At the end of Asitabarna's narration, chief-whip Deepankara left his seat, got up and said: "That Amrapalli is today Baisali's terror, a living curse, an anathema. I wish she died the death of a vermin and let us live in peace."

Convener Ganadhara asked: "But where is Amrapalli?"

Suddenly, the symphonic music of her anklet was heard outside the palace, with its rhythmic echoes and reverberations filling the empty air with its enthralling, jingling cadence. Unclear, seething voices rose from the assembled crowd: "Here comes Amrapalli. Here comes Amrapalli."

Amrapalli was blue-bodied; her soft and spongy feet were dyed with reddish hue in a design that looked like the scattered congregation of pomegranate seeds; her thin waist was covered with a golden string that elongated up to her thighs like a sonorously downflowing cascade; her arms and breasts were embellished with golden jewelleries; below her curved eyelids were placed two undulating, drunken, deer-eyes; they looked like the limbs of Madana's[4] bent, curvaceous bow.

Deepankara admonished: "The republic of Baisali lies endangered only for this contemptible beauty, Amrapalli. States like Bideha, Malla and Kalama are all madly hankering after this accursed beauty. Are you cognizant of the fact dear commoners that the enormous wealth of this poor gardener's daughter can even ridicule Baisali's huge and unmatchable royal exchequer? If our secret information is correct, the Magadha king Bimbisara, being irresistibly enamoured by this virgin's enthralling beauty, contemplates abducting her into his palace. Everybody of us would be aware that it's not entirely impossible for an incorrigible lecher like Bimbisara whose anecdotes of habitual debauchery is a universally known phenomenon. If Bimbisara continues with his salacious advances towards Amrapalli, then a military conflict between Baisali and Magadha is inevitable for Baisali would definitely resist such mean, salacious and indecorous advances by this despicable usurper. But of course, its dire consequences are also not hidden from us. For how long Baisali's small military establishment can sustain itself in front of the unsurpassable might of the gigantic Magadha army? So, it is my humble and sincere supplication to all of you that as per the customs of the land, let Amrapalli be declared a public-courtesan before all. For the finalization of this proposal, I solicit a referendum."

---

4   Madana is the God of love and lust in Indian mythology.

Like a deer being afraid of the hunter, Amrapalli stared at the assembled citizens with her eyes overflowing with heartrending effluxes of pity and terror. At this point, another member Silabhadra got up and said: "This voting is not required at all as this proposal is unanimously acceptable to all, without even an iota of doubt; I believe even Amrapalli won't gainsay this proposal. It is mooted by the revered commoners for safeguarding the safety and sovereignty of Baisali."

Thus, the proposal for a formal voting was readily repudiated by the assembled commoners, unanimously. Amrapalli's compulsive conversion to a public-courtesan was authenticated and ratified through mass clapping and raucous howlings.

The convener Ganadhara intervened at this juncture and said: "Esteemed members of the union. With your kind permission, I henceforth declare Amrapalli as a designated public-courtesan. Her beauty is her crime."

II

During the time represented in this narration, this was the practice in states ruled by communities like Shakya, Koliya, Bideha, Maurya, Buli, Kalama and Bhaga. The virgin whose beauty caused conflict between kingdoms, territories and communities was forced to become a public-courtesan, or rather, a public whore. She was made available for civic consumption and thus, unwarranted conflicts between kingdoms and territories could be readily averted. Similarly, that day Amrapalli was declared a public-courtesan in Baisali, in the mentioned commoner's assembly. But it cannot be undermined that she was still a remarkably intellectual lady of the Buddhist times and the anecdotes retelling the saga of her intellectual competence are legion. In *Theri Gatha*[5], one finds her touchy and tearful autobiographical anecdotes delineating a public courtesan's pitiful plight during her time. One sees how during the mentioned period, a public courtesan was treated as no more than a readily available sexual material for the common populace. It recounts, poignantly, how that day, Amrapalli sacrificed for Baisali all the pleasures of her life — the pleasures of her womanhood, the bliss of her motherhood, her aspirations for a joyous, exuberant life — everything.

However, the public whores during the mentioned era were not simply consumable sex objects; rather, they possessed the highest degrees of competency in literature, music, dance and many other arts and crafts. In addition, their wealth and affluence could ridicule those of the kings and other royal personages of eminence. In the Buddhist text *Binayapittaka*, we can peruse the biographical details of Kashi's illustrious courtesan "Ardhakashi" whose one night's income equalled the royal exchequer's one day's revenue. But since she could not procure customers at such high price, she had to half her price. Thus, from that day onwards, she became known as "Ardhakashi."

III

Amrapalli's gaudy and sumptuous bedroom in her palace in Baisali! She lay half-conscious on her heavily cushioned cot, after giving birth to a gorgeous and attractive baby boy. Her maidservant Sirima stood beside

---

5   An ancient Buddhist text containing autobiographical poems by women poets.

her with the baby in her lap, and intended to say something to Amrapalli.

Sirima called: "Elder sister."

Amrapalli opened her exhausted eyes with great diffidence and said in a harsh, repudiating and contemptuous voice: "Why do you stand there Sirima? Go and throw that baby on the roadside. It will be morning after a while."

Sirima retorted: "What a beautiful, princely baby! It looks exactly like King Bimbisara. I don't feel like throwing him away, elder sister."

Amrapalli's tormented motherhood lifted its subdued head again, and her voice softened for a moment being overpowered by the natural benignity of compassionate motherhood.

Sirima told in a softened voice: "Take the child onto your lap, elder sister. Take the child onto your lap."

But Amrapalli's mood altered suddenly and she screamed like a trampled serpent: "No! No! That's a blasphemous child, a trammelling incarceration for me. An abominable curse of this life! Go and throw him out right now, Sirima. I would have kept her if she was a girl child. But it's a baby boy. Go and throw him right away. I don't want to listen to your futile arguments anymore, Sirima."

The baby started crying inconsolably on Sirima's lap. Amrapalli shouted: "Press the cloth in his mouth Sirima. Let him be finished. Why do you stand here? Go."

Sirima pressed the baby closer to her breast and left, with a sullen and grumpy face. Amrapalli felt like taking revenge on herself, on an abandoned and neglected life that she lived in the midst of the brooding despair of a begrimed and feculent whore's life.

But why did these streaming tears flood across her schmaltzy eyes? She could not have afforded to be so weak, so vulnerable, so emotional, so mawkishly sentimental. After all, she was a courtesan, a public whore.

IV

By an incredible stroke of destiny, that day's abandoned child of Baisali later on became the famous Ayurvedic[6] physician Jeebaka—Gautama Buddha's disciple. But of course, there is no chronological record in History that recounts, with credible evidence, the growth and nourishment of this abandoned, nameless, and parentless child into a famous physician in the hands of a childless man.

V

Many years later . . .

Amrapalli's whorehouse remains pathetically empty and people-less. Her spring-tree-like body, once suffused with the pullulation of wealthy and ensnared lechers, has now become pale, haggard, desiccated. They have left for younger Amrapallis. She is now sick with an incurable disease; her emaciated body is fully paralyzed, and incapacitated. In her dancing feet, there prevails the dull and sombre inertness of rocks; in her once flashy and

---

6   An ancient medical practice in India involving the treatment of diseases through herbs and other arborescent materials as medicines.

shimmering golden body, there is the dark and terrorizing reign of death. A cataract has invaded her deer-eyes, like a pervasive, irremediable mildew. Padmabati is now Baisali's new public whore. Everywhere, one hears her praises, eulogies and adorations, as if there was no Amrapalli ever in that region.

VI

On the sick bed, lay Amrapalli's filthy and diseased body, like a lifeless and abandoned object. Jeebaka sat beside her and rubbed some balm on her eyelids. Amrapalli shouted like a mad woman in distress and screamed in an anguished and grief-stricken voice: "Give me some poison Jeebaka. I don't need this life. I know Jeebaka my lost youth won't come back; my lost vision shall not return. Your efforts are futile, Jeebaka. Your efforts are all futile."

Jeebaka rubbed his hand delicately on her forehead and told in a cosy and consolatory voice: "Be quiet mother. Rest assured. I shall bring back your youth; I shall bring back your health."

Jeebaka was blessed with a magically alleviating touch in his hands. His words never turned out to be false and inconsequential. Amrapalli had unbounded confidence in his immaculate, curative prowess; she had completely surrendered herself to him. "Oh! What solace! What calmness! There is wonder in his hands. What affection do I feel when he utters the word 'mother'!" Amrapalli told herself and desired to see him even with her blinded eyes. But for her, everything was hazy and indistinct, like blinding layers of thick and condensed fog. For a moment, she remembered the day when she held the baby in her breasts and felt the limitless joys of contented motherhood. She felt the same joy today with the divine touch of Jeebaka's calm, soothing hands on her diseased body.

Amrapalli asked; "Who are you Jeebaka?"

Jeebaka answered: "I am a beggar, mother. I am a beggar. Without being perturbed, you take a nap, mother. I assure you will be completely cured, very soon."

Amrapalli was not yet amply convinced with Jeebaka's confidence-providing words of reassurance. She retorted: "But this is not your true recognition Jeebaka. Tell me who you are."

Jeebaka emitted a rhapsodic flicker of smile on his face and answered: "The identity of a beggar is that of a beggar, mother. He does not have a father, a mother, a wife, a son, a daughter and a world of his own. He is only a beggar. He is liberated from all obligatory worldly entanglements."

Amrapalli responded in an affectionate voice: "Sit beside me for a moment, Jeebaka. Oh! My eyes pain severely. Rub your calm, soothing hand on my shrivelled, desiccated forehead once more, Jeebaka."

Jeebaka obliged like an obedient child. A deep satisfaction and a calm repose filled Amrapalli's inside being like Lord Buddha's palliative and consolatory blessings.

Jeebaka, while rubbing his hand on her forehead, said: "This is the ultimate truth of this world, mother."

Amrapalli asked: "What truth, Jeebaka?"

Jeebaka answered: "This disease, this old age, this infirmity, this fret, this suffering! Youth is transient and evaporative mother."

Amrapalli asked: "Then what?"

Jeebaka answered: "This world is an illusion, a tantalizing mirage, mother. Desire is the cause of all grief and suffering in this mundane, sublunary world fraught with fret, disease, decay and afflictions. Renouncement of the world is the only panacea, the only pathway towards ultimate liberation. That is why the prince Sakya Singh[7] is a monk today, a happy and contented denouncer of the world.

Amrapalli asked: "Who is that Sakya Singh?"

Jeebaka said: "I shall tell you his story today."

******

Amrapalli was slowly recovering through Jeebaka's recuperative treatment and care. Her vision had not yet completely returned; yet, she could see everything, though a little hazily and unclearly.

That day when she first saw Jeebaka, she felt as if her heart was extirpated with a hunter's acuminous arrows. This Jeebaka—a beggar! If her abandoned child lived, he would have resembled this Jeebaka, this angelic Jeebaka, this godly alleviator of the pain and suffering of the sick and the diseased. The same appearance! The same vast and sprawling forehead! The same twinkling, glittery pair of eyes! The same sword-like nose!

No! No! Why should Jeebaka be this filthy Amrapalli's bastard child? He is a god, a reincarnation of divinity, a godly saviour of tormented mankind. Oh! What

---

7   The prince of the kingdom of Kapilabastu who later on renounced the world and became Lord Buddha.

sense of un-fulfilment! What hunger! What desire! What desperation to clutch him in her lap! Two streams of glitzy and glittering tears flew down form Amrapalli's eyes, while glistening flashily in the crimson light of the setting sun.

Jeebaka asked: "Are you crying mother?"

"No! No! Why do you call me mother? Call me Amrapalli; call me a whore; call me by whatever foul and feculent name you prefer." Amrapalli answered. But could she not be called a mother? If her own son sat beside her sick bed, if he spotted tears in her eyes, he would have certainly asked: "Are you crying mother?" But here was Jeebaka who had sacrificed everything for the 'Sangha[8],' who had relinquished every banal and telluric pleasure of this earthly life for salvation.

Jeebaka asked again: "Are you crying mother?"

Amrapalli wiped off her tear with her saree and said: "No Jeebaka! There is slight pain in my eyes."

Jeebaka assured her with his calm and comforting words: "You don't worry, mother. The pain shall subside."

Amrapalli responded: "Yes Jeebaka! You had promised me that day to tell me the story of Sakya Singh. Tell the story now."

Jeebaka started narrating Amrapalli the story of Sakya Singh.

VII

Gautama Buddha shall come to Baisali.

The news has spread through the city's every nook

---

8   The Buddhist religious community.

and corner, like internecine, wildfire spreading unstoppably through a jungle.

The Lichhabbis are busy welcoming the Lord as per their customs and conventions. Baisali's men and women are ecstatic and desperate to see him, to get his blessings.

In the meantime, Jeebaka has completely cured Amrapalli and restored her normal health and wellbeing. With Jeebaka's godly, curative treatment, she has regained her youth and splendour, just like a moon being freed from the demonic Rahu's[9] bewitching and fatal clutch. But a deep and pensive thought, a sordid realization of something baleful and augural has descended upon her clear, luminescent eyes like the pervasive shades of pithy, dark clouds; some unspeakable grief has swindled away their wealthy lustre.

Jeebaka asked: "Do you know mother? Lord Buddha is coming to Baisali."

Amrapalli answered: "But how useful is that news to me, Jeebaka? I am a filthy whore. My body is an object for sale. For public consumption. Am I sanctified enough to confront the holy Buddha?"

Jeebaka retorted with a curious smile: "Who is not a whore mother? Your body might be an object for sale. Not your soul! But those who have made their bodies and souls cheap, sellable objects, are indeed more abject and despicable. These Lichhabbis of Baisali! Have they not compromised with their conscience in the name of 'dharma'?"

In both the eyes of Amrapalli, danced the lucent, dazzling flames of scorching summer.

---

9   It is, according to Hindu mythology, a devilish power that engulfs the moon in the dark-moon night.

Today, King Bimbisara shall arrive in Baisali. Magadha's messenger has brought the news.

Today Buddha shall come to Baisali.

There is an unprecedented commotion in Amrapalli's palace. Every corner is decorated with attractive and odoriferous clusters of flowers; their captivating and winsome aroma has spread through all directions like the sedate and voluptuary Earth's unctuous and seductive odour. Amrapalli told old Sirima: "Today, shall arrive the guest, Sirima--the long-awaited guest."

The full-moon evening of spring! Amrapalli's orchard at Baisali's outskirts is filled with the enthralling fragrance of innumerable, mango buds. After many days, Baisali has decorated herself in the beautiful and sensuous attire of an ornate and bedecked bride awaiting her man on a gaudy, flower-embedded, nuptial bed. Chandra was Amrapalli wear the anklets over her ankle, the golden thread around her dark, slender waist, and the golden bracelets around her smooth, dusky arms. Sirima was spraying her hair with intoxicatingly aromatic perfumes. Holding a dazzling mirror in her hand, Amrapalli laced a lustrous and effulgent tinge of vermillion on her forehead.

Everywhere there is an ear-splitting commotion; today shall arrive king Bimbisara.

Like a joyous, exuberant river dancing elatedly on the rocky pavements of a hill, Amrapalli's heart throbbed with an abundance of joy and exhilaration. For today shall arrive the Buddha, her long-awaited guest.

Amrapalli shouted in an excited voice: "Shyama, Chhanda and Sirima! Don't delay any more, friends. The full-moon-night's moon blooms in the sky like a golden lotus, emerging from the darkened silt of Earth. Look at its crimson petals. Look how they spread and diffuse into the dense, inebriated evening air; look how they steep every earthly thing in its crimson colouration." There was frenzy and excitement in her voice.

Sirima decorated Amrapalli's wig with florid and glitzy clusters of dazzling Ashoka[10] flowers.

The highway roiled with the deafening noise of the amassed, bustling and rambunctious crowd. Amrapalli frantically ran towards the window and peered at the outside world booming with noisy, blusterous festivity. An attendant rushed in and said in a gasping intonation: "Madam! King Bimbisara waits for you in the luxury room."

Lord Buddha is arriving in Baisali. Its citizens revel unrestrictedly with mirthful joy and exhilaration.

Amrapalli came rushing in from the window and screamed elatedly: "Hey! Here comes the guest, Sirima! Let this luxury items be abandoned here."

Amrapalli sprinted outside like a crazy woman. Her dishevelled strips of hair flew in the air like thin clusters of disjointed clouds hovering listlessly across the bluish firmament of a trenchant sky; from her hair, fell many Ashoka flowers, intermittently on the ground, filling the desiccated air with their bewitching fragrance.

The poet's violin stopped. King Bimbisara rubbed his eyes with surprise and disgust.

Baisali's royal whores were left speechless.

---

10   A beautiful flower that blooms on the plant of *Saraca asoca* in the Indian subcontinent.

The Buddha lifted his deific, shimmering hand into the air to bless Amrapalli, in her ostentatious and glitzy Luxury chamber. Her gorgeous and dandified attire looked conspicuously pale and lacklustre; Buddha's glowing face sparkled with divine splendour and luminosity. Amrapalli prostrated on his feet like a felled tree. The disciples sang in a chorus:

"Buddham saranam gacchami,

Dhammam saranam gacchami

Sangham saranam gacchami"

(I take shelter in Lord Buddha,

I take shelter in the holy religion,

I take shelter in the holy community)."

*****

The Miner

It was drizzling lightly.

Enshrouded by misty, white clouds, the bleary top of the Karo Mountain was half-visible. The bell of Bird Company's mine rang with an ear-splitting and raucous clang . . . It was 12 o' clock.

On one side of the railway track, Janam Munda sat on a coal and manganese powder-heap and kept staring at the front road with vacuous, unblinking eyes.

Janam Munda was an old man. If someone enquired about his age, he would respond offhandedly: "I don't know." But if one went on nagging ad nauseam, then he would say: "May be forty." But in all fairness, he looked no less than sixty. His unkempt hair had all turned bedraggled and grey. His eyes were horridly swollen and were continually watering. His flat nose-tip looked like an obnoxious lump of flesh accumulated on his dusky-complexioned face. On his dark face, the large nose looked clear and prominent and elongated outward like a sharp-edged sword. Around his waist was wrapped a piece of begrimed, dust-ridden mine-cloth and around his head was wrapped a similar smudgy, grey-coloured cloth like the worn-out residue of a putrescent turban. In the murky cavity between his ear and his head, was stuck a half-burnt cigarette with a darkened, haphazard tip. Francis Hansda had offered him a cup of tea and one cigarette in the Badbil market.

Francis kept instigating him that if he went to the Padre Sahib, he would offer him money, clothes and also will gift him a piece of fertile land. Janam Munda would spend the rest of his life in peace, prosperity and happiness.

"What nonsense!" Janam retorted with vehemence and continued: "I would never leave my "Bada Bonga[11]" like you. How many days would I live more? There is nothing more in my destiny. I would never leave my Bada Bonga."

Janam Munda was the revered headman of Karo village. He had two daughters—Raymani and Phulmani who brimmed with the splendours of full-blown youth and their dusky, scintillating bodies had become attractions for every youthful passer-by. Their sweet smiles flew through Karo Hill's ravines like swift, golden rivers gurgling and frothing while meandering languidly through the winding, rocky terrains of the mountain. Their faces glowed like the resplendent moon of the full-moon night while their dark, supple bodies resembled two dazzling effigies adroitly carved in granite by a dexterous stone mason. Janam Munda thought he would have gotten twenty oxen as 'sukhmu[12]' by getting his daughters married to two able-bodied Munda

---

11   A tribal god.
12   Bride-price. In many tribes it is customary that the bridegroom's family has to offer bride-price to the bride's family. This is exactly opposite to the dowry system where just the reverse happens, i.e. the bride's family has to offer money as dowry to the bridegroom's family.

men. But perhaps that was not in his destiny fraught with poverty and irrevocable wretchedness. Now there was no use going to that Padre.

Clad in the overarching shades of the Sal trees, the grey road curved like a serpent sliding sluggishly through the mountain's rocky and curvilinear trajectory embracing distant places like Inginijharana, Jorda, Kouda and Banei. On that road ran innumerable trucks and jeeps flashing their luminous headlights on the colossal bodies of the giant and immovable hills that sat haphazardly, like antediluvian statues clad in the kimono of evening mist. At the back of the driver's seat, there stood the tribal girls holding the truck's railing in their hands. There were beautiful, wildflowers stuck on their heads; their lips were flooded with uncanny smiles and their dark, agile bodies were stuffed with the deluge and efflux of full-blown youth. In the jerky movement of the vehicle, their deft bodies undulated lavishly while flaunting the overflowing abundance of their shimmering youthfulness.

Janam Munda's daughters Raymani and Phulmani might also be moving inside a similar truck gliding ruggedly through the winding, gravely roads along a distant hill's rocky pavements. They were no more visible to Janam's blurring vision; neither did he elicit an urgency to see them anymore. They had become abominable miners in the greed of new sarees and costly perfumes; they had gleefully offered themselves to company sahibs and Punjabi drivers for the sake of money; they had compromised with their purity and dignity, unabashedly.

Janam Munda won't care if they went to Hell. How long shall he live more? He was being watched by Burubanga of Thakurani Hills, Birabanga of the Sal jungle,

Nagera of the Kara River, Hasabanga of the lowland and above all, Rimilibanga of the whole forest region[13]. He couldn't have left them for the Christian Padre. Janam paid soulful obeisance to these gods by genuflecting on the ground and then touching his forehead on the same.

A lone and empty goods train came rushing in towards the Badbil railway-crossing from Jamda station while whistling vociferously. The engine emitted thick and condensed volumes of fuliginous smoke into the air; the smoke coiled like an airy snake and congealed spirally into the atmosphere's expanded, smoggy and frosty reservoir. The empty wagons were loaded with soil impregnated with ores; they were carried to the Calcutta Port from where they were exported abroad through the voluminous ships that dragged their giant, metallic bodies on the bluish surface of the sea like pestilential, untidy roaches. Gold and dollars flew indiscriminately into the company-owners' pockets in exchange; they relished with the plundered wealth of the soil and the forest, like bloodthirsty beasts relishing on the flesh of the slain preys. The consecrated soil which the tribal men worshipped as Hasabanga and the sacred hill which they adored as Burubanga were now being excavated and looted by the foreign companies; they had become mere commodities and sources of heavy dividend for these obnoxious bunches of savage and importunate traders who meant only business, and nothing else. The green hill on which the jungle god Birabanga roamed in the middle of the night playing his flute was now blasted and excavated and was left as a barren, treeless plateau, bereft of the dense, green foliage overhead that enshrouded the pious, and consecrated soul of the forest like a soothing, velvety cover. The god Birabanga who blessed the verdurous soul of the

13   These are different tribal gods.

forest awash with greenness was now being brashly sold in the inclement and 'whores-infested' bazaars of Calcutta like a cheap, inexpensive commodity. These modern, civilized interlopers had plundered everything—the consecrated soil, the beatific, 'fern-crowded' hills and Karo's exquisite natural environ where the gods of the tribe cohabited with their impassioned and dedicated devotees—the clean-hearted tribesmen. They had looted Janam Munda's dazzling, refulgent sweat, his pure and unadulterated tribal blood and also the pious and untarnished dignity of tribal virgin girls like Sunia, Kainta, Raymani and Phulmani. After everything had been outrageously plundered and looted, the hill and the land lay barren and forlorn in the midst of a treeless, shrub-less, marooned wasteland, from whose slaughtered body raised a twirling, greyish whirlwind of dust, like an ugly, evil spirit.

Raymani had eloped with a Sikh driver; Phulmani had become a prostitute in the Badbil slums while suffering from venereal diseases like Gonorrhoea and Syphilis. Janam Munda sat with an empty stomach on a manganese dust-pile near the railway-crossing, shed tranquil tears from his sunken eyes and looked vacantly at the cold unconcern of a blithesome sky that was tumbling on his head like a crushing weight from heaven.

Janam Munda was not just a denizen of the Karo village, but also was a glaring symbol of exploitation and torture.

Wagons after wagons were loaded with Bird Company's manganese ore and with Tata Company's iron ore. They were dragged by the scraggy and destitute tribal men and women labourers and were finally clamped to the railway engine that yelled with an ear-splitting noise and emitted volumes of serpentine smoke into the air. Soaked with the poisonous smoke, the wild flowers stuck on the women' heads dried up and looked like crumpled, desiccated paper-made flowers whose dampened and greasy petals stunk malodorously rather than emitting a cool, succouring fragrance. And then came a sudden cloudburst; it drenched the women's bodies dripping with sweats; the sweats mingled into the pouring rain's torrential deluge. Their wetted breasts beneath their half-torn, semi-transparent sarees looked arresting and prominent and could not evade the predatory traders' ever-watchful, hungry and lustful eyes.

Oh God! So much of beauty! So much of hunger! So much of plenitude! So much of poverty! They were all possible in the dark, mining regions of Odisha.

Janam Munda wanted to get up and move. The Karo village was a long way from here; it glimmered like a tantalizing and distant isle in the flooding sunlight of the luminous sun. During the days of sowing and harvesting, the villagers worked in the corn-fields and during off seasons, they worked in the mines. Some of them managed to get jobs there whereas the others had to return empty-handed. But Janam, and in fact, all of Karo's villagers abhorred the mines for they thought that they were the places of exploitation and to work there was nothing but a sordid compromise with their dignity and self-esteem. That is why the mine-owners often had to outsource workers.

Of course, these days, the scenario was no more bleak and discouraging; it had changed dramatically and the mines had become attractive places to work. One easily got cut-price liquor from their canteens, cheap cigarette from the adjacent Badbil market, and inexpensive perfumes and low-priced, colourful sarees from the same place. That is why, these days the workers, instead of abhorring the place rather relished working there, out of their own sweet volition. Yet in places like Karo, Khendra, Dalki and Belkondi, some villagers still apprehended to enter into the mines' dusty, repugnant and malefic compound for certain irrational, unfounded, yet conventional prejudices. For them, whoever went there became an abominable miner. Some strange rumour ran in these tribal societies that the mine-owners slaughtered some workers and offered them to Burubanga, and chopped off others' limbs.

Last year, the whole region was terribly affected by drought. Whatever crops Janam grew in his small piece of land was all annihilated by the devouring drought's all-encompassing, diabolic tongue. His lush green field that once pullulated with crops dancing in the soughing wintry wind had now turned into a barren, desiccated and famished wasteland.

But today the contractor refused point blank that there is no work. Eating some scanty boiled rice in the morning, Janam came to find some work in Badbil; but he did not get any. Karo was a long distance away. Janam got up to move.

II

The liquor shop at the end of the Badbil slum!

It was the weekend wage-time for the miners as the next day was a Sunday and the mine remained closed. The road was flooded with drunkards merrymaking in the middle while singing vulgar songs and displaying obscene gestures towards the indecorous tribal girls accompanying them. There was a scuffle amongst themselves; their recklessness knew no bounds and was flaunted in the mid-road in the form of a loud, noisy and unpleasant hullaballoo. The obscenely dressed tribal girls accompanying them kept on laughing puckishly at their rascally show of rowdiness and by the next morning, the whole week's income was splurged. What was left was only one kilogram of rice, and nothing else. The importunate womenfolk had already reached to extract money from their drunken husbands; the roadside pulse-vendors had arrived with sticks in their hands; the trade union's hooligan had also reached the spot for his quintessential 'chanda[14].' A huge rambunctious, clattering crowd had gathered in front of the liquor shop as if to reinitiate a clangourous, drunken carnival there in the dark. Broken clouds had dispersed all along the sky like floating fragments of butter in un-churned milk making the latter look like a gigantic, pinkish, embroidered canopy in the faint, glimmering moonlight. The vagrant moon peeped through their fissures while hovering in the sky like a drifting, shining saucer. A few drunken men had already started their frenzied tribal dance beating tin-drums at the shop's dark and dingy backyard.

Man Singh Munda walked languidly out of the shop with an alcohol-bottle squeezed in his armpit's dark and sweaty cavity. He was not particularly enjoying the ruckus made by the unruly crowd on the gloomy, chequered open landscape outside the shop lying outstretched like a tattered and perforated dirty carpet. He only wanted to drink alcohol quietly in a tranquil atmosphere in the brooding darkness of the jungle, at a distance.

Somebody called his name loudly from within the crowd. Man Singh looked back.

---

14   Colloquial term for fees.

A Gorakhpuri[15] hooligan came out flaunting his obnoxious, shadowy, wide, dust-ridden chest with enormous vainglory. He was a new recruit into the Company and was hired from outside to work as a professional bouncer. He wore a pair of torn and ragged black trousers dangling like the slender torsos of two wild trees and a dirty banyan around his chest. A square-shaped locket hanged from a black thread around his neck like an ugly, sinister design carved on a stygian, muscular body. His legs tottered under an alcoholic spell and he swayed languidly like a drunken bear when he walked.

That day Man Singh had gone there with a resolve to bring Phulmani back from that Hell. But she had employed this hooligan to beat him up. But Man Singh beat him instead for which the latter was seriously injured and was hospitalized. Being a strong and athletically built able-bodied man of the Munda tribe, Man Singh possessed the hideous strength of a tiger. Who could beat him up?

Today the Gorakhpuri Narayan Prasad wanted to take revenge. He started scolding Man Singh using filthy and un-parliamentary slangs.

Man Singh looked back and stared into the prolonging depths of Narayan Prasad's drunken, vacuous eyes for a moment, and then, threw a solid punch on his flat belly. Narayan tumbled onto the murky ground with a shriek that mingled into darkness like the surrounding jungle's low, indistinct whisper. Man Singh snatched Narayan's stick from his hand and lifted it into the air to smash his head. But the next moment, he threw it away with a disdainful gesture of condescension and vanished into the jungle, soundlessly.

---

15   -From a place called Gorakhpur in North India.

An unknown wild flower's ambrosial fragrance spread through the atmosphere like an odoriferous smell emanated from the colossal jungle's lush, green body. A restless cuckoo sang mellifluously from within the enshrouding dense foliage of a nearby mango tree. Man Singh sat on a moon-blanched clearing on the roadside, leaned dolefully against a Sal tree and stared deeply into the mysterious quietude of the moon-light-bathed jungle.

This golden moonlight reminded him of Phulmani, about the Indar[16] festival of older days. This Phulmani! A contemptible whore! She is dead by now. But what is the use remembering her? Man Singh dispelled her intruding thoughts from his mind and started ruminating over his own past while taking large sips of liquor from the bottle. His eyes had turned blood-red and he felt a sharp sting of pain in his plaintive heart—a pain that started flowing though his swollen veins like injected doses of venom.

He remembered his village, and his thatched, mud-house that floated in his memory like the shadowy fragments of a fractured dream. He lived in the village named Dalki. They had a little house on a small hill at the village-end. Man Singh's mother had painted its walls with a lot of care . . . first a layer of grey soil, than another layer of black soil and finally a third layer of yellow soil. Above was a roof of tiles. During this time of the year, the house got surrounded by fields filled with a pullulating crowd of green popcorn plants.

Today, that house is broken and streaks of greyish and blackish darkness ooze out like droplets of blood from its battered and wounded body. Man Singh's father died in

16   -A tribal festival where men and women dance holding each other's hands.

the battle in Assam where the Padre had sent him to fight the insurgents on behalf of the govt. forces. At the village-end, his mother placed a stone under a Sal tree as a dull, sublunary remnant of her deceased husband. Two years ago, she was eaten up by a tiger in the jungle into which she had ventured to collect some wild fruits. Man Singh put another three-cornered stone near his father's stone. In spring, the flowers fallen from the deciduous Sal tree enshrouded them all into invisibility.

Man Singh was lost in his thoughts . . .

III

Many years ago, Karo village celebrated the Indar festival with unbounded excitement and vigour. The Sal jungle was filled with reddish 'Palash' leaves that spread through the greenish canvass of the forest like a locomotive calligraphy. Drunk with 'mahulo,'[17] the young men and women of Karo, Dalki, Khendra and Belkondi danced in concentric rings to the tunes of the drum's thumping sound and the flute's symphonic music, while clasping each other's hands in tight, passionate grips. When their feet got tired dancing, they eloped into the jungle in pairs holding each other's hands and clung to each other in tight, concupiscent embrace. And then they roamed like errant souls unleashed on Kara River's sprawling sandbank that stretched like an unfolded, white carpet rolling alongside the streaming river—the river of eternity.

The nomadic moon had soared high up into the sky like a golden-winged eagle. Today was the time for love, for

17   -A wild flower blooming in the forests and fermented to make alcohol by the tribal people.

merrymaking, for amorous togetherness, for unmitigated rampancy.

The long day ended with the approaching evening. The moon had risen deep into the sky as usual. Man Singh kept playing his flute while looking unabashedly at the streaming emptiness of the distant horizon. Phulmani kept dancing with the other Munda girls; their waists and shoulders were joined together like beads of an undulating string. They looked like a bunch of aromatic, wild flowers swaying randomly, together in gentle wind, tossing their decorous heads to and fro in a wavy, vermiculate tracery.

Man Singh stopped playing his flute for a moment, walked towards Phulmani, coiled his right hand around her slender, supple waist, dragged her closer to his chest and kissed her on her cheek. Phulmani smiled mischievously for a moment, gave a gentle push to Man Singh and ran into the jungle like a dark shadow gliding across the long stretches of the moon-blanched sand. In a moment, she congealed untraceably into the jungle's surreptitious depth; Man Singh followed her with the frantic desperation of a lunatic lover and spotted her near a giant stone. He clasped Phulmani from her back and lifted her into the air. Phulmani kept paddling her denuded legs in the air for some time with counterfeit gestures of resistance while at the same time getting enamoured by the sweaty smell of Man Singh's sturdy, macular body. She was getting arrested by the ensnaring hypnotism of the latter's hurried breaths. Man Singh placed Phulmani on that giant stone and said: "Hey Phulmani! The moonlit night looks beautiful. What do you say?"

Phulmani smiled impishly again without uttering a single syllable, slept for a moment on his bared, hairy chest, and started scratching its skinny surface gently with her sharpened, dye-ridden fingernails. And then, she ran swiftly towards the river bank, sat on a shallow stone-pedestal and kept watching the vagrant moon swim across the river's calm water like a dazzling goldfish.

In the gently soughing spring-wind, there was the intoxicating fragrance of the 'mahulo' flowers.

Man Singh told in a loud voice: "Phulmani! I shall marry you." His voice ricocheted from the stony walls of the surrounding hills and filled the empty nocturnal air with its thumping reverberations.

Listening to his words, Phulmani chuckled mischievously again and ran across the river bank into further depths of the forest. For a moment, it seemed as if she merged into the streaming river at a distance and flew across its curvy trajectories into the midst of the blinding mist and fog lying ahead, interlaced in an inextricable mess.

Man Singh searched for her for a long time, and finally traced her on the bank of River Kara, beneath a Sal tree. From a distance were audible the relentless beating of drums and the mellifluous songs of the Indar festival. Phulmani kept humming a similar song. Man Singh sat adjacent to her and asked: "What song are you singing, Phulmani?"

Phulmani did not respond at all and kept humming the song heedless of the latter's enticing proximity. She was like the moon-blanched Sal forest; she could be touched, but could not be fully comprehended. Holding her in his arms, Man Singh put a vermilion mark on her forehead expecting that Phulmani will reciprocate. But she did not do anything of that sort and ran away into the village without giving any desired response to his earnest propositions.

IV

The alcohol from the bottle was not fully consumed by Man Singh yet; he slipped the bottle into his pant-pocket, absentmindedly, and kept dreaming about a pensive past that kept on haunting him like an irksome ghost. He was still left with a week's wage. Lighting a cigarette, he headed back towards his village with unstable steps, accompanied by the pithy and condensed darkness that walked alongside like a friend, a companion. He wanted to be thoroughly drunk today, drunk to the lees.

But there was a time when Man Singh abhorred liquor to an extent that he did not even intend to touch the bottle; its very presence for him was repulsive, nauseating. He kept himself at an arm's length from the drunkards and did not appreciate the obnoxious practice of drinking at all. He also abhorred the mines to the extent that he never stepped into its filthy, repugnant and despicable premises. But the day when Janam declared that he won't give his Phulmani to him unless he offered him ten oxen as 'sukhmu,' he was left with no other choice but to step into the accursed, dusty terrain of the mines. With unrelenting hard work through prolonged days and nights, he accumulated pi after pi.

But perhaps it was not in his destiny to get the money.

That year the whole area was afflicted with severe drought; there was not a single drop of rain for months together. Every procured food items from the jungle including wild fruits and seeds were all exhausted. Some people still managed to get some more of them from the jungle and survived on them for a few days more. The Karo villagers usually did not go to work in the mines unless there was dire necessity. But this time, they were left with no option but to enter into its dreary and sepulchral premise that they abhorred so much and always looked indignantly at. But Janam Munda stuck to his manly vainglory and muttered to himself with a proud and intrepid heart: "It's absolutely fine if I shall die without a single morsel of food; but I shall never step into the dank and clammy premise of that monstrous Hell. I am the son of this forest. I am the son of this soil. I have lived here. I will die here."

V

Phulmani sobbed intermittently while sitting alone inside the house that resembled an abandoned dark cave, an abysmal pit. Above, there was a dilapidated roof made of broken brass and tin. And on the roof, were randomly placed broken bricks, stones, fractured bicycle-rims etc. such that it was not blown away in an abrupt, stormy wind.

Even the cruel and pitiless moon did not spare her. The inside of Phulmani's hut was awash with moonlight flooding from the sky and streaming onto the pebbly floor through the dilapidated roof's fissures. It fell on the rain-water-filled gutter and on the incongruous scrambles of rotten mosses all around and also on Phulmani's gonorrhoea-afflicted, sick body. While shivering in high fever, she felt as if the cruel and savage moonlight stabbed her on her belly; she felt like shrieking in excruciating pain, but all in vain.

These days she gets high fever every evening. The next morning, she re-freshens herself with heavy dosage of alcohol, laces her face with aromatic talcum powder, puts clusters of wildflowers on her wig and wears a dazzling, multi-coloured saree to attract the customers. Nowadays she roams with a six-feet-tall Punjabi truck driver who looks like a demon from Hell and drives a truck without license. He earns hundred rupees per day. Some days, he goes to distant villages like Noamundi, Chaibasa, Chakradharapur and Koida to transport goods from the company and comes back to Karo village in the blinding depths of the night. He meets Phulmani near the alcohol shop where both drink alcohol and eat roasted chicken in an adjacent 'dhaba.' Then he carries her into the dark dungeon of a hellish, abandoned hut where he makes love to her like a beast. He squeezes her tightly in the inescapable barricade of his sturdy arms and stinking chest, undresses her in mad desperation, licks her dusky, fleshy body with his devilish, salivating tongue dangling out like that of a rabid dog, eats morsels of her flesh with brutish delightfulness, and pounds her hard on a half-broken cot that creaks bizarrely every time he forces himself into her. Reduced into a crumpled lump of flesh in his beastly arms, Phulmani keeps losing her essence in that darkness, woven around her like a tortuous and entangling net.

Today that Punjabi driver has beaten her black and blue under the heady spell of liquor. He doubts of having contracted some venereal disease from her. But Phulmani did not cry for the pain of her body, but for the invisible scar that was festering gruesomely inside her mind, was gnawing her soul like an avaricious beast.

She remembered Man Singh Munda; his apparition floated before her eyes like an indistinct flicker of an image; she remembered their amorous moments of proximity during the Indar festival celebrations. She could have married him and have lived happily ever after roaming in the forest, living on the wild fruits, seeds, dancing uninterruptedly in the immense festivity of many blissful springs.

But that year a heavy famine grasped Karo; its villagers had to go to the mines to get some work. Phulmani's sister Raymani went to the mine along with the villagers. Janam Munda admonished her time and again that in the mines, they slaughtered the labourers and offered them to Burubanga; they chopped of their limbs and threw them into the dark pits outside as fodder for Hasabanga. But Raymani didn't give a damn and went to the mines.

But Phulmani did not come with her. She waited for the day Man Singh gifted ten oxen to Janam Munda and married her.

VI

It was a dark and cloudy evening in Karo filled with the soft, cloying, aromatic breeze of the zestful and exuberant autumn. Phulmani boiled some wild bitter-potatoes in an earthen pot which Janam Munda had procured from the forest. But they never lost their bitterness even after repeated boiling.

Raymani came back from the mines and sat a little far away from Phulmani. Janam, drunk fulsomely with rice porridge, lied almost unconscious on a dilapidated cot under a gigantic, shady Sal tree. The trance-inducing fragrance of wild flowers emanated from the forest's mysterious, atavistic body had hypnotized all living beings into dizzy spells of an inexplicable frenzy.

But another fragrance emanated from Raymani's dusky body—delicate and awful fragrance.

Phulmani asked: "Wherefrom comes this sweet, soothing aroma, Raymani?"

Raymani started chuckling in a drunken voice while Phulmani kept staring at her— speechless, bewildered, flabbergasted. She did not wear that old, grubby and worn-out saree anymore and what she wore instead was a garish, flamboyant and red-coloured one. She had delightfully stuck ornate and resplendent blobs of sweet-smelling wild flowers in her wig and had laced her face with aromatic talcum powder.

Awestruck, Phulmani asked in a befuddled and flustered voice: "Wherefrom did you get these, Raymani?"

Raymani, while continuing chuckling frolicsomely, took out a small perfume-bottle from within her saree and handed it over to Phulmani, casually and languidly as if it was a small and negligible thing that she gifted her with easefulness and she possessed things which are more costly and precious. The latter held that bottle close to her nose and felt its honeyed, assuaging fragrance, deep within her craving, prehensile soul. She was delighted. Like a magician, Raymani took out a piece of scented soap and a mirror from within her saree and flaunted them before Phulmani's dazed and flabbergasted pair of eyes. Phulmani swooped onto the mirror within the flash of a second, snatched it from Raymani's hand and looked at her face, narcissistically, in the hot, reddish streaks of light gushing out from the blazing furnace and radiating across her dusky and resplendent face. She couldn't imagine she was so beautiful. Enamoured and beguiled by her own splendiferous beauty, she didn't even know when the hot, steaming water from within the pot had evaporated and the boiling bitter-potato inside it had turned into a dark, putrid mass of charcoal.

She asked again, with an urgent tone of clamant curiosity: "Wherefrom did you get these, Raymani?"

Raymani answered while laughing insolently: "The mine-owner gifted me all these. He has promised to give more."

The next day Raymani and Phulmani were found walking towards the mine, hand in hand, arm in arm, chuckling, laughing, and merrymaking while buzzing and serenading melodious tribal songs and lullabies.

From that day onwards, Phulmani has slept with many contractors and has been deserted by many, innumerable times, of course being priced for the wilful violation of her modesty and chastity. Man Singh Munda has managed to buy ten oxen and has come on multiple occasions, to Janam Munda's house asking for Phulmani's hand, repeatedly and earnestly. But each time, she has kicked him away showering on him throngs of scathing and vituperative tribal slangs.

Of course, today the times have changed. The mysterious allurement of the mines has also vanished. There are times when Phulmani craves, desperately, to run into her mud-house in her village Karo, and congeal into its fostering, life-giving darkness, like an affection-craving child congealing into her mother's spongy, absorbent, and consolatory arms. She wishes to drink the lurid, fragrant autumn breeze to the lees and pacify her parched and tormented soul with the mollifying and comforting embrocation of a reposeful and assuaging calmness. Long ago, she had brightened the greyish, lacklustre walls of her house with tinctures of resplendent colourfulness by smearing them in layers with black soil and red soil brought from distances. But today she is an accursed outsider, a filthy, abominable whore.

Phulmani looked at the gravelly road that stretched and coiled into the distant horizon like a winding arc. She got enamoured by its soothing invitation, as if it would carry her back into her cradle, into the blissful days of her joyful adolescence, into her dreamy and delirious past . . . The road led to her Karo village. But suddenly she felt as if it was filled with thorns and in a fit of tremor, she looked beneath.

Gosh! She was bleeding from her feet, profusely. Phulmani shrieked in terror and buried her face in her hands. The next moment, she looked at the road again, but did not spot a single thorn. She looked down at her feet; she didn't bleed at all. With the gradual recession of the nightmarish reverie, she got back to her senses and gazed insensately into the farthest limits of the sky overhead. She looked into its bottomless excesses of emptiness and felt as if her inside 'being' was morbidly empty, like the sky itself; it contained no feeling, no emotion, no sentiment, but only a chilling, marauding vacuum inside.

VII

The bell clanged in the mine-owner's house. It was twelve o' clock in the night. A ghostly calmness had percolated through the dark night like a snake's venom. The clouds had slowly accumulated in the sky and the peripatetic moon had leisurely waned in their midst like a golden bird waning in the midst of clumsy assemblages of enshrouding foliage. Drunken to the throat, Man Singh stood in the darkness outside Phulmani's house in the hope that one day she would accept him, that one day she would extend her dusky, voluptuous arms in an welcoming gesture to cuddle him, and he would fling himself into her inviting body in a momentous fit of joy and ecstasy.

But that day for him was a day of startling revelation. While anxiously loitering outside Phulmani's cottage awaiting an affirmative response from her, Man Singh Munda surprising heard her whispering to somebody and then suddenly bursting out into piercing and tumultuous peals of laughter in the dark. He crawled closer to the door like a stealthy leopard and peeped clandestinely through a little fissure to see the mysterious occurrences inside the chequered gloom of the cottage's dimly lighted, obfuscated space. But what he witnessed was beyond his wildest imagination. On the floor, lay that Gorakhpuri hooligan Narayan Prasad with his enormous limbs spread out against the floor like a felled tree's strewed branches. Phulmani slept lavishly on his chest and kept laughing maniacally as if being possessed by an uncontrollable whim, a strange and inexplicable delirium. There was not a single cloth in her body. She went on beating Narayan Prasad's chest with her relentless fists in a frenzied rhythm and started laughing obstreperously again, like a mad woman possessed by a ghost. A broken lantern with a cracked glass-cover lying abandoned at the corner emitted streaks of diffusive, dim lights into the room's overarching darkness; they made things sparsely visible to Man Singh. Two or three unlabelled, country-made liquor bottles lay scattered on the floor.

Narayan Prasad had not yet forgotten the nagging

and excruciating pain in his bones caused by Man Singh's beating that day. He kept contemplating that one day he will finish him off if he got an opportunity and then, shall bury him somewhere inside in an abandoned pit in the mines. With clenched teeth, he shouted: "You Man Singh . . ." Hearing Man Singh's name from his mouth, Phulmani started roaring like a lioness and told Narayan Prasad: "You are a neuter. You are only a man of words. You come to me the day you kill him. Now don't show me your ugly, cowardly face and get lost from here."

It seemed as if there was no peace in Phulmani's life till Man Singh was alive.

Narayan Prasad boasted: "See girl! You will see how I shall finish that man off. Every evening he returns from the Rungta market through the Thakurani Road. One day, I shall hide myself in a roadside bush with an axe in my hand, and shall finish him off in one stroke."

Narayan Prasad started roaring like a lion.

Listening to Narayan Prasad's words, Man Singh's blood coddled like sizzling hot water sloshing fiercely inside his throbbing clusters of veins. Without wasting a minute, he gave a solid and thunderous kick on the door; it opened from inside with an ear-splitting bang. Looking at Man Singh's violent, monstrous figure materializing ominously right in front, Phulmani shouted: "Man Singh! You go from here. Otherwise, I shall call the police."

Without uttering a single word, Man Singh rushed, hysterically, to the corner of the house, picked an axe lying out there and stood before Narayan Prasad and Phulmani while staring at their aghast and frozen eyes with the unmatchable vengeance of a wounded tiger. Narayan

Prasad understood the gravity of the situation and intended to tame Man Singh by jumping onto him and capturing him promptly in the barricade of his sturdy, muscular arms before the latter could do anything outrageously fatal. But before he could do anything, Man Singh severed his head in a single, monstrous blow. Streaks of fresh blood were splayed all along the floor and a few slashes also fell on the dimly flickering lantern's cracked, dust-infested glass. While screaming, Phulmani tried to rush out of the house, captivated by the craven terror of imminent death standing right in front of her in the form of Man Singh turned into a bloodthirsty demon. But before she could escape, Man Singh held her by her hair, threw her on Narayan Prasad's body and cleaved her head into two halves with another blow.

With two severed heads in his hands, Man Singh surrendered before the police.

VIII

It was raining cats and dogs that morning. The rain did not stop at all. It was a dampened, swampy and cloudy Sunday. The mines were closed.

Janam Munda kept ambling errantly across Kara River's banks while catching glow-worms. He had not eaten glow-worm curry for a long time. When his daughters lived with him, they used to bring a lot of these to make tasty and delicious dishes for him. Janam Munda used to salivate looking at the seething congregation of these glow-worms in the air.

He had already placed folded Sal leaves near the anthills' holes. Within a blink of his eyes, these folded leaves were filled with hundreds of glow-worms. The clouds thundered intermittently over the Thakurani Hill. Kara River's darkish waters brimmed with great profusion and rushed towards the sea, towards eternity.

Somebody shouted from behind: "Hey Baba! Hey Baba!"

Janam looked back. Karkanda Munda of his own village was running frantically towards him. He worked in the Badbil mines.

Karkanda reached near him gasping vigorously and said in a breathless voice: "Phulmani's body lies there in the police station. Go and bring her. Last night, Man Singh has murdered her along with that Gorakhpuri hooligan, Narayan Prasad."

Janam looked at Karkanda's face--dumbfounded, flabbergasted; then, he kept looking at the Thakurani Hills like a thunderstruck lunatic. He had forgotten catching glow-worms.

IX

It was customary in the Munda tribe to cremate the body. Phulmani's pyre was slowly getting extinguished by the gently blowing breeze on Kara River's banks. The darkening clouds kept accumulating in the sky in throngs and clusters. On the brimming waters of the river, Phulmani's funeral fire danced elatedly like the jungle's daughter Phulmani herself.

Janam Munda looked at the Thakurani Hill at a distance and ruminated: "I have lost everything. What else remains here?"

He thought of leaving the Karo village. But where would he go? Singhbhum? That was also a place full of mines. Banei? It was also the same there. Pallahada? Would the contractors have left any jungle uncut there? Who knows?

Janam Munda knew it right. Whoever goes to the mines, never comes back. Burubanga kills him or her by sucking their blood. If you disrespect Burubanga, would he not kill you? He could not imagine why his Phulmani and Raymani chose the path of destruction? Janam looked at the jungle again. There were times when the peacocks danced in this forest and tigers roared from distances . . . There was a time when Burubanga roamed here in the depths of the night playing his flute and everybody listened—the mesmerized forest, the dumfounded trees, the dancing peacocks, the passing clouds and the astounded moon-- everybody. Now in the depths of the night, one hears only the hellish sound of axes cleaving through the throbbing, terrified hearts of trees that were turning into insipid, dead pieces of wood. The land is plundered; the hills are destroyed; his Raymani and Phulmani are gone. Before that, he had also lost his wife. Tears jerked in his eyes.

Phulmani's pyre was completely extinguished now. Janam collected a handful of ashes and a few pieces of bones from the ash-pile as the last surviving remnants of his dead daughter, and kept walking towards his village while a calm and unflustered expression of an angelic stoicism had precipitated onto his stiffened, metallic face, quite visibly. There was no emotion left in his heart. It was dry, dispossessed.

The next day, he dug a hole near his dead wife's grave beneath the Sal tree and filled it with Phulmani's ashes and bones that he had gingerly collected from the ash-pile. Then he lifted a shining, three-cornered stone and placed it on the hole. A few Sal flowers fell on the stone like tear-droplets from his eyes.

Janam Munda believed that this old Sal tree is Burubanga's consecrated abode. But the savage contractor has already marked it with tar. In a few days, it would be felled by his axe. Janam prostrated on the ground, paid obeisance to Burubanga, and then started walking in an uncertain direction, away from the tortuous saga of plunder and exploitation of the civilized world. While leaving, he looked once at his wife's grave and once at his old, dilapidated hut. In his blurring vision, the road stretching ahead looked to him like a dark, desiccated and waterless river—the river of time--meandering languidly into the misty depths of the frosted horizon—the horizon that is nothing but a thrown away fragment of eternity into which everything dissolves—desire and memory and this filthy, decaying body. Janam had no idea where his own grave would be.

He wiped out tears from his eyes. Trucks after trucks kept racing towards the Koida mines. Janam kept trudging into the unknown depths of the jungle...

*****

The Dance of the Ghost

While moving through the main line, there is a small station called Madhupur on the borders between Bihar and Odisha. I had missed the 64-Up and was waiting to catch 72-Up Madhupur Express and my travel-destination was the above-mentioned station. If the train was on time, it would have arrived at 7 in the evening. It was five more painstaking and strenuous hours of patient waiting for me. The waiting room was small, crammed and dingy and did not offer any conceivable note of joy or excitement for the waiting passengers whose crumpled faces looked cumbersomely sad, loathsome and haggard. Who comes to Madhupur these days? Its golden days are over and today it is an abandoned, forsaken place filled with stale reminiscences of a glorious but faded memory.

But in its heydays, lots of rangers from Calcutta and Patna visited Madhupur during Durga Puja or the Christmas vacations and spent happy and pleasurable times amongst its attractive and delightful natural vista, and amongst its warm, endearing and clement environment. Many of them, gotten enamoured by Madhupur's beautiful, temperate climate, its long, sprawling, green fields, its shady and succouring Sal forest and its adjacent, blue, and wavy Hazaribagh mountain-range, had constructed here attractive residential houses and palatial bungalows thereby converting the place into a marvellous, residential as well as holidaying hub. A huge rangers' colony was established in Madhupur due to the large and teeming influx of these regular and persistent vacation-time visitors and the place was particularly crowded by the swarming assemblage of these rangers' families during Puja and Christmas vacations. But these days, the new generation of affluent rangers travels to places like Srinagar, Darjeeling, Kalimpong, Goa, Calangute Beach, Mahabalipuram or Delhi to enjoy their vacation, being enamoured by the illusory grandeur of these big, honorific names. For them, Madhupur is no more than a deserted place, a forsaken slum.

Last year, I felt an irresistible urge to spend my vacation in Madhupur. I had a sheer and fascinating attraction for this place—an attraction that persisted in my memory like an awestruck adolescent's delirious fancy for a woman's body. Instead of staying in three-star or five-star hotels like this new generation of affluent men, I contemplated spending my vacation, quietly, inside an ancient, grass-infested, desolate building bereft of the gaudy flashiness of a furnished mansion. Madhupur's untraceable throngs of shifting shades and its intricate traceries of curvy and criss-crossing roads leading to the blue and wavy Hazaribag Mountains had mesmerized me, like unexplored spaces of an enchanting dreamland. A friend of mine had thankfully booked for me an antediluvian, dilapidated and moss-covered resort here where I thought I could comfily spend my desired days of queer and enjoyable holidaying. On a marble slab stuck on the resort's shabby and ramshackle gate, you could still find an unclear inscription written in Bengali: "Madhu Kunj."

After the first day of my stay, nevertheless, I was captivated by a feeling of intense boredom and depressive monotony. The place's empty and mysterious silence had in a way slaughtered the initial romantic buoyancy and exuberance with which I had arrived here with my excited mind pullulating with innumerable dreams, fancies and reveries about the place. By staying here, one could readily comprehend the difference between the tantalizing and illusory Madhupur glimpsed through the moving train's window-railings and the actual Madhupur lying out here—ashen and charmless—lousily outstretched across a swampy, abandoned wasteland. It is a clear and indisputable reiteration of the same, age-old distinction between illusion and reality—one a fanciful imagination and the other, a crude and unambiguous manifestation of irrefutable reality!

In the condensed evening fog, the distant mountains looked like hazy and cracked fences.

There were two ghostly houses lying adjacent to my resort and the third house after them was an old and antiquated one, inhabited by a retired judge. The overt expressions of antiquity overflowing across the grandiloquent but ramshackle texture of the house created an impression as if it belonged to an antediluvian, prehistoric era. The aged gentleman lived here alone. Of course, the only other beings living with him were a dark-coloured, imbecile-looking cook and a brooding dog whose reddish tongue dangled perpetually from his mouth like a spacious, rubicund curtain. Two houses away from his, lived an ex-landlord in a huge, palatial mansion. Like the retired judge, he also lived there alone, amidst throngs of memories—disjointed and hallucinatory—of his bygone days of affluence and might; those days had receded like fizzling-out waves of a plummeting ebb. He was certainly a mysterious creature; he never interacted with another human soul and was hardly seen coming out of his mansion.

Hotel 'Parvati' was the only place where you could fortuitously encounter a few ghostly human faces in the morning, in the noon and in the evening. If you looked at these people carefully, you could trace invisible masks of stoic indifference planted on their ceramic faces; they looked like weird and obnoxious-looking aliens from a distant, unexplored planet hovering somewhere untraceably in our vast, empyrean galaxy—the Milky Way. Engrossed in their own mysterious aloofness, they exhibited neither excitement nor exuberance.

*****

In the waiting room, I kept dreaming of so many fascinating things about Madhupur. While carelessly shuffling through a detective novel's pages, I sensed that a gentle lady sitting right in front and weaving a gorgeous woollen fabric threw at me strange, innocuous and stealthy glances, uninterruptedly. An urgent and outlandish curiosity flashed across her eyes like lightening flashing across a cloud-infested sky whereas a thin, sepia-tainted smile played on her lips like the exuberant spring's gentle, pacifying breeze. She was perhaps waiting there for an approaching train. I no more had the age neither did I have the youthful friskiness to enjoy a mature lady's ensnaring stare at me in such a calm, depressive and reclusive environment. At an age of above-fifty, my dishevelled, greying hairs flew over my head like sundry 'Kasatandi[18]' flowers undulating, with childish freakishness, across

18   -It is a white-coloured Indian sub-continental flower.

the vaporous and shimmering canvass of the steamy, drifty air. While shaving every day, I could spot on the brownish surface of the dust-infested mirror, a scourging army of deepening frowns ravaging across my blotchy and slackening cheek. It was a clear and irrefutable testimony of my dwindling youth and approaching old age. These frowns had freakishly intensified the skinny and wrinkly stubbornness of my ageing face.

The gentle lady kept on knitting wool with a downcast head. I kept shuffling through the pages of my detective novel.

*****

If I continued staying for two days more in that obnoxious haunted house in Madhupur, the proliferating aloofness in my acutely embittered mind would have snowballed into a deleterious ennui and would have driven me mad, without doubt. Two days ago, I met in Hotel Parvati a dreary gentleman who, despite his modest and ostentatious demeanour, looked to me like a thoroughgoing cynic; he curtailed my spirit by initiating a bizarre, depressing and tedious conversation with me and I had to listen to him willy-nilly, unwittingly. He was a local. I developed a casual acquaintance with him during that dull and not-so-exciting interaction over a cup of tea, and while talking, the gentleman smoked a branded, fashionable cigar and left out twisted, serpentine curls of smoke into the gloomy and condensed evening air. He told me: "With so many beautiful places around, why did you choose to come to this abandoned, swampy wasteland called Madhupur? Do you have a genetic strain of madness running across generations in your family? No sensible and well-meaning man ever comes for holidaying to this empty and marooned place these days and an educated, well-meaning and well-informed person like you stepping into the dark crevasses of this abandoned Hell is beyond my honest comprehension. Have you ever come across, at least accidentally, these two rarefied and antique specimens of humanity—that judge and that landlord, these two self-obsessed, maniacal creatures? They hardly emerge from the ensconced spaces of their secluded chambers and interact with people around. Two local lads had once chivalrously ventured into the judge's house to collect some 'chanda[19]' for the Jagaddhatri[20] Puja." Wearing a multi-striped 'lungi[21],' he hounded them out holding a large, terrifying stick in his hand."

Thankfully, I never visited this esteemed judge's abode for a gentle gossip, uninvitedly. But once out of an ad-lib curiosity, I had almost reached his building's entrance, unpremeditatedly, but was thankfully dissuaded by the repellent masses of weeds in his primeval garden and the ugly, scrunched face of that old, mossy and primitive building that giggled at me, spitefully, like a monkey. I came back hurriedly as if I had confronted a scary ghost.

The gentleman said again: "Didn't you find another resort other than 'Madhu Kunj'?"

I answered: "Actually, my stay in this bungalow was arranged by an old friend from Patna. I did not have to pay any rent except some meagre tips to the watchman."

"O! Engrossed in the gluttony of free accommodation, you have wilfully chosen to put up in this old, antiquated

---

19   -Some monetary contribution.

20   -A goddess in Hindu religion.

21   -A long-clothed attire for Indian men.

building bereft of the shiny freshness of a new and sophisticated, modern residence. But don't forget that after sunset, you won't confront a single soul loitering around in this enchanted landscape. Even, the old, local inhabitants of Madhupur, who are well-acquainted with every nook and corner of this locality, fear moving along its front road, once darkness sets in." The gentleman told in a shuddering voice, as if a dark veil of craven terror had enshrouded his scrawny, crumpled face.

I remembered how astoundingly the watchman had reacted that day when I handed to him my Patna friend's letter recommending my stay in 'Madhu Kunj.' I did spot a bizarre and obnoxious glare sweeping across his befuddled pair of eyes and could sense an uncanny strangeness floating fulsomely in his quaint and spooky response. He told in a sugary and kind-hearted voice that elicited the note of a highly sentimentalized, motherly concern: "Sir! If you confront any untoward difficulty or inconveniency whatsoever, please summon me, without the slightest of inhibition. I will be right up there at your service; in fact, I can stay in the bungalow throughout the whole night if you so wish. Sir, as you can see, this is an antique and forsaken bungalow containing nothing but a darkened void inside; I must not refrain from letting you know that there are multiple, weird and horrifying anecdotes floating in the air about this mysterious and enchanted bungalow. In fact, I myself have heard some of them from various mouths; they have sent scary waves of tremors and trepidations across my shuddering spine. That's why I am telling."

The watchman slept there on the bungalow's veranda during my prolonged and disillusioned stay of four nights in that marooned, sepulchral and obfuscated graveyard. He spent sleepless nights there in the brooding darkness, most of the time squatting on an old, decrepit bench at midnight while peering eerily into the shimmering darkness, without a thought, without a feeling. I often asked him out of effervescing curiosity: "Hey man! Why do you sit on the bench through the whole night instead of sleeping?" He answered with an unsolicited gesture of benignity: "Dear sir! Since you are a newcomer here, I am a little concerned about your safety, security and well-being in this godforsaken, deserted place. But you don't worry. I am always there for your help." I conjectured that the flooding deluge of sympathy that had swept across his pimple-ridden face like a spanning wave was for nothing but some handsome tips. I told myself: "Let him sit there for the whole night. What is my problem?""

I had asked that gentleman in Hotel Parvati: "Sir! Everybody is afraid of Madhu Kunj. Is it a haunted house?"

He had explicatively narrated before me the enchanting story behind Madhu Kunj's mysterious and esoteric conversion from a happy abode bustling with noise and vivacity into an enigmatic, haunted house overnight: "A few years ago, an old Bengali lady stayed here with her daughter-in-law and a few servants who performed their household chores. Both were widows. One day for reasons unknown, the daughter-in-law bolted the room from inside and committed suicide by hanging herself from the ceiling. After that scary incident's unfortunate occurrence, her mother-in-law departed for Brindavan permanently, and never returned. From that day onward, the house lies completely empty and abandoned; it has gotten converted into a frightful haunted house fuming with frightening wisps of gloom and darkness and nothing else. On rare occasions, of course, the mother-in-law's relatives do come and stay here for a few days and go back leaving the house empty and abandoned once again. A lot of people have confronted the daughter-in-law's ghost roaming across the area in ominous, moon-blanched nights, sometimes weeping and sobbing, sometimes laughing fiendishly at the occasional passer-by filling the empty air with its echoes and reverberations while at other times, singing a beautiful, melodious lullaby—a lulling, lethal death-trap. At times, she is found standing on the middle of the street, without a dress, stark nude."

But I must asseverate, proudly, that I never feared ghosts. So the story probably had very little perceivable impact on my unperturbed psyche and it was hardly able to fluster my unruffled temperament. But for a moment, I thought that perhaps this is why the watchman slept every night on the veranda with a lantern burning beside him, throwing innocuous streaks of gloomy rays into the blinding depths of the night—a night that wanted to devour it like a sharp-clawed and sharp-teethed, sinister beast. But again, I thought that he took that risk, camouflaging his own, innate fear of ghosts, only for the sake of receiving some handsome tips.

But does a human being live after his death? If no, then how could people witness that dead lady walking on the street, stark nude, in serene and clammed-up, moon-blanched nights? This was all rubbish, all rumours and unsubstantiated hearsays. I never believed in such puerile, moronic and airy ghost-anecdotes that are fundamentally unfounded, fanciful and misleading by their very nature. But the gentleman, while flicking the cigarette's ashes into the emptied teacup, said with an uncharacteristically grave and serious intonation: "Listen mister! You may not believe in such stories, and brush them aside by calling them sheer claptrap and balderdash. But don't forget that like some troubling and distraught memories that keep haunting us disturbingly, there are also some dead human beings that return into our midst as ghosts. Without being able to sever the sublunary ties with their previous births, they return recurrently into our midst as ghosts to relive their unfulfilled lives and to accomplish their unconsummated desires. Those that have been able to attain salvation do not, of course, come back."

"This is another mad man." I said to myself.

I did not argue further with the gentleman.

*****

I kept on shuffling through the pages of the detective novel in the waiting room.

But the gentle lady was caught unawares this time. She kept on staring at me, stealthily and was confident that with my attention overwhelmingly buried in my book's pages, I was not really catching her furtive and investigative glances directed at me and my calm, composed and unflustered countenance. But I did notice her nagging, clandestine activities, secretively and all on a sudden, lifted my head and looked straight into her eyes. Without being able to deflect her glance with an unanticipated suddenness, she was caught this time—unawares and red-handed. Then she gently smiled at me and said: "Can you not recognize me Nikhil Babu? You are Nikhil Chaudhury, right?"

I was stunned, flabbergasted. How could the gentle lady know my name? Did I have a previous acquaintance with her? The strange familiarity in her mature voice and the easy intimacy flooding across her cajoling stare thoroughly perplexed me in that little, embarrassing moment. The same deep chasm in her left cheek when she smiled!

I said impromptu: "Hey Kalyani! You are here. How strange!"

Kalyani was my classmate in college. During our student days, women's education had not flourished considerably. In our class, there were only a few girls, Kalyani being one of them. She said in a sullen and grumbling voice: "Ok! You did not recognize me, right! You all men are congenitally afflicted with this terrible malady called 'forgetfulness.' You do not take time to forget. You forget even your friends in a moment."

"A moment . . ." I snorted in the form of an instant and spontaneous response to her tenuous allegations. Then, I gently retorted: "Thirty-five long years are a moment for you, Kalyani!" and continued: "How could have I prognosticated that we shall meet here in this godforsaken, marooned waiting-room after so long? But how come you are alone? Where is your mister?"

A wry and dispassionate smile floated abruptly on Kalyani's lipstick-ridden lips and she said: "I have no mister, Nikhil. I am still Miss Kalyani Das, History Reader in Muzaffarpur Govt. College."

Now I realized that her sunken forehead was bereft of a dazzling vermilion mark, neither did she wear jinglingly flashy and elegant bangles around her wrist. There was also no decorative and embellishing golden necklace dangling around her neck, emblematic of a glossy and opulent married life. I mustered some courage and asked in a slightly apprehensive tone: "Is it due to some vow or for the sake of some spiritual pursuit, Kalyani?"

Kalyani answered promptly: "Well! You can say any of these. But you know pretty well that I was never interested in getting entangled in the abstruse intricacies of bothersome family life."

But how could she know that only for her sake, I had mugged up R. N. Tagore's poem "Kalyani" that day:

In the bower of flowers is thy matchless abode

O heavenly harbinger of beauty and prosperity!

Thou remain busy in your chores evermore.

I struggled to recollect the following lines; they were lost in time's circuitous labyrinth.

My friend Kuna parodied these lines and gleefully taunted me:

Alone is your abode in the midst of hawthorn fences.

Hey Kalyani! Thou remain busy in History Honours

class evermore.

Kalyani stopped knitting wool and started gossiping with me, loquaciously, digging out slaughtered memories from within the dark, dingy graveyard of time. She said to me: "I can see you have not yet relinquished your typical, juvenile habit of mindlessly shuffling through a book's pages. Do you remember that despite not being a History-honours student, you still frequented the Library to attend to History seminars? It was funny and intriguing for us girls. You used to open a History journal and hurriedly shuffle through its wasp-infested, yellowing pages; but I only knew that you didn't peruse even a single line. How could

I have ignored the fact that you were actually a student of English Honours?" Saying this, Kalyani started chuckling at me, which within a split-second, turned into a loud and boisterous laughter whose echoes and reverberations were heard inside the waiting room's stuffy, obfuscated space.

Oh God! Kalyani observed my freakish, romantic ventures with such avid keenness and unsullied precision. I had absolutely no idea. But I was certainly Kalyani's diehard lover. But, of course, that love remained unexpressed and consequentially, unreciprocated. Firstly, I was a pathetically shy and introvert guy, and more so, our society during those days was meagrely considerate and permissive, particularly in the matters relating to courtship between adolescent boys and girls.

That is why I could never tell her with a softened, mellifluent, and cajoling intonation: "Kalyani! I love you."

I was lost in vainly scrambling through these discombobulated arrays of past memories; but I did realize, immediately, that it was not a viable occasion for such hollow, sentimental recapitulation of forlorn memories and a futile, imaginative re-enactment of bygone events and episodes of my life. Meeting Kalyani, perchance, after a prolonged gap of many years was no more than a mere, fateful coincidence, a fluke, a serendipity. We could not also have discussed our families, as we had none, neither were we keen on engaging in vibrant political discussions. If I was a student of History, we could have perhaps discussed a few important historical events and episodes.

But I was an English-Honours student and I won't deny, of course, that I used attend History seminars, regularly, only to see Kalyani, to lose my fidgety 'self' in the protracting depths of her cowering, curvaceous eyes, to have that rare, conceivable feeling of completeness in her cool, succouring presence in my vicinity. I could recollect, even now, how my yearning heart beat uncontrollably in that languorous afternoon, enamoured by Kalyani's sweet, enthralling beauty.

But my friend Kuna did notice my perennial inability to fall in love and taunted me: "Which girl will ever fall in love with a coward like you?" Amongst our contemporaries, Kuna was an illustrious and acclaimed lover. I had seen him regularly receiving blue-coloured love letters from an unknown beloved, perhaps an exotic princess from a faraway dreamland. At times, I got jealous of an adroit and unfailing lover like him who could make a girlfriend with the blink of an eye and I was such an ineffectual novice."

Kuna told me again: "How can a coward like you ever impress a girl?"

Of course, I was an incorrigibly shy guy and was not adept in such queer and quixotic ventures into the dicey and perilous amphitheatre of obsessive courtship. But I had not hesitated to ask Kuna: "Then tell me what can I do to impress a girl?" Kuna promptly answered: "You have to be a little glamorous, a little chivalrous as girls envisage glamour and chivalry as men's most rare, treasured and adorable possessions. If one day you can muster some courage and hold Kalyani's hand in yours and say: 'Kalyani! I love you,' she would definitely reciprocate, and reciprocate unhesitatingly."

But I asked Kuna with a quivering voice laden with a momentous concern and apprehension: "If she complains before the principal?"

Kuna responded a bit snobbishly: "There is risk in everything in life, my friend."

His words still reverberated in my ears like a distant echo.

The cloudless autumn sky tumbled into my eyes in white, translucent splinters through the waiting room's open window. A light, white cloud drifted along the sky like a fuzzy and disjointed memory from our unfulfilled past; I could see it navigate through the air, right in front of my eyes, like a torn-away piece from my disgruntled heart.

I asked Kalyani: "Oh! I forgot to ask you about your destination, Kalyani. Patna or Hazaribagh?"

She answered: "I am waiting for 77-Down-North Indian Express. I will be going to Durgapur. My uncle stays there."

I breathed a deep sigh of relief. It was already 4 o' clock. 72-Up Madhupur Express was set to arrive in the platform at 7 pm. Of course, if it was on the right time! Like the gentleman in Hotel 'Parvati' confronting the denuded lady's ghost on the streets of Madhupur in flashy, crimson and moon-blanched nights, I was now witnessing the ghost of my past dangling in the mid-air, right in front of me, like a hazy and indistinct apparition. In a whimsical recollection of my past, I tried to recapitulate the extent of my desperation for a little proximity with Kalyani, years ago, during those fanciful days of my failed romanticism! The sheer thought of it perplexed my mind. I wondered whether we are all mere, inconsequential playthings in the hands of unsurpassable destiny, worthless like clusters of trinkets and gimcracks. When time's fleeting background shifts, also shift our action, our thought, our behaviour, our whole life—a life that is a compendium of uncertainties created by the ever-shifting and whirling flux of time. This realization came to me abruptly, like a sudden denouement, an epiphany.

I was deeply engrossed in my quiet, outlandish philosophizations, when Kalyani readily interrupted and said smilingly: "I cannot control my laughter when I remember that day."

I answered absentmindedly: "Which day, Kalyani?" I muttered inaudibly: "Your and my histories are tragic ones, Kalyani. Of course, now, they might look comic."

But she had not forgotten that incident: "Why were you so nervous that day, Nikhil? Your face that day . . . It looked so outrageously funny and clownish." Saying this, she started laughing puckishly again while looking at my face with a slanted and impish gesture.

"Nervous! When?" I asked in a curious voice.

Kalyani became garrulous and said: "You came that day to the History seminar and shuffled through the pages of an archaeological journal while throwing sporadic, stealthy glances at me in the midst of the seminar's noisy, bustling hullaballoo. Grossly terrified, you breathed so heavily that I could hear its reverberations from a distance. And then, all on a sudden, you ambled towards me with hastened steps like a wrecking tornado and I buried my face in the History book of Sir Jadunath Sarkar, while blushing in embarrassment with a downcast head. With a panicky voice that clearly lacked confidence, you asked for a pencil for taking notes and without lifting my head, I quietly handed it over to you while purportedly avoiding frontal eye contact with you. But I could readily sense that you wanted to touch my finger, instead, and in attempting that (which in my comprehension was a preordained one, and perhaps instigated by some adroit lover-friend of yours) you dropped the pencil on the ground as your hand was shaking viciously. Not being able to hold my hand, you left the place bearing on your face a glowering and morose disposition."

It was indeed Kuna's formula that I wanted to apply on Kalyani. I had strategized to press her hand in the guise of borrowing the pencil and then, profess my love with manufactured expressions of grace and easefulness. But it was an incredible disaster when it came to the actual performance; I was thoroughly discomfited and humiliated. If someone could portray my chagrin on stage, it had to be none other than the great Charley Chaplin. But of course, Kalyani's funny recapitulation and ludicrous narration of the episode after years of its actual occurrence looked hugely awkward and disconcerting.

I no more wanted to listen to her narration with its funny and preposterous nitty-gritty details. So, to divert attention, I said: "Oh! It's very hot and humid today. These people have not even placed a table fan here for the passengers. They boil inside the waiting room like cockroaches, lizards and frogs boiling inside the cauldron of the Shakespearean witches. It's a bitter irony that these railway officials barefacedly pontificate from the high altar of official and moral accountability, and deliver unending harangues in the name of passenger- amenity."

Even Kalyani could spot reddish tinges of discomfiture blooming on my face like red roses in a garden, and readily refrained from venturing into that incident, any further. She buried her head down and kept knitting wool as if there had never been a conversation between us, thus far.

A bell rang breaking the waiting room's silence.

The bearer dashed into the room and said: "77-Down North Indian Express is arriving. This is the second bell."

I was assured that the train would arrive at last.

Kalyani's soliloquies that had continued so far like the Phoenician sailors' endless navigation across the bluish firmament of an endless sea had come to an abrupt halt. After a few minutes of breath-taking pause, she suddenly extended her right hand towards me and said: "Please do a bit of fortune-telling, Nikhil. You were a great palmist, right?"

"I was of course practicing palmistry and mesmerism etc. those days as a hobby, as a strange fascination that was born out of nowhere. But how could you know that?" I asked Kalyani.

She said: "The way you boys loitered around us, we also kept track of your activities, man. More so, I had so many times spotted palmistry books in your hand. Were you a serious palmist or what?"

Without responding to her juvenile inquisitiveness, I quietly held her right palm in my hand and perused the lines with utmost care and precision—the lifeline, the fate-line, the wealth-line . . . But I had truly forgotten the finer arts of palmistry, of course, due to my lately developed disinterestedness in that art, and also, due to invincible time's murderous, all-effacing sweep through the hazy and unclear terrains of my fragile memory. Holding Kalyani's hand in mine was no more a delightful and exhilarating experience, as it would have been a few years down the line. I felt very cold and apathetic with the placid touch of her toughening, desiccated palm on which her greenish veins and arteries intercepted and crisscrossed in an imperceptible and mindboggling mess. It was rather a gruesome feeling of utter discomfiture that I felt in that touch; the brooding, depressing evening on the top of it made her presence dull, unexciting and wearisome. With a feeling of ineffableness, I left her hand and said: "I have forgotten palmistry long ago, Kalyani. Is it so that a human being's destiny is written only on his or her palms?"

I could sense that she was a little hurt by my words.

Now, the third bell rang.

Kalyani came out of the platform holding an attaché in her hand. A yellow vanity bag dangled from her left arm like an inchoate reminiscence from our hazy and irretrievable past that had mysteriously followed us through time's eternal, all-embracing flow. Then she said to me: "Ok! Bye! Who knows when we will meet again like this, suddenly?"

I also walked a little distance to say goodbye to her, as an officious marker of courtesy and gentlemanly sophistication. 77-Down North Indian Express waited for three minutes in the platform and left. After a few minutes of heart-throbbing commotion, the platform came back to a standstill, to its original stoic silence, to its calm and unperturbed tranquillity in the midst of the enormous drift of things around. Human faces poured in, diffused into the platform's smudgy, sepulchral space, collided and mingled to form a clumsy confluence of hazy and splintered faces and then dispersed around like disjointed, sordid images of the ailing modern men.

My train was to arrive two hours later. There was not even a tea stall in the platform. Absentmindedly, I walked alongside the railway track for some time, only to get rid of my nagging boredom and cantankerous monotony.

The afternoon-shade had gracefully descended onto a 'Palash[22]' tree, right in front. The tree looked to me like a female ghost, a denuded female ghost, like the one the gentleman in Hotel 'Parvati' frightfully witnessed on the abandoned streets of Madhupur in moon-blanched nights. Now I was witnessing the denuded, fiery ghost of my past right in front of me, in broad, pervasive daylight. But it did not surprise me anymore, neither was I terrified by its sudden, freakish inception. The ghost grew bigger and clearer, taking an ugly and ferocious shape in the mid-air. It looked at me with cruel, pitiless and taunting expressions; it ridiculed me by throwing a flurry of indistinct banters and sarcasms; it tried to terrify me by flaunting its grisly, grotesque monkey face. But all in vain! I showed my monkey face too and giggled at her like a vengeful adolescent. But it was an interesting encounter indeed. I could have never forgotten that. With a quiescent and restful sobriety planted on my face, I kept walking.

The ghost kept dancing horridly in the mid-air . . .

*****

---

22   An Indian sub-continental tree with beautiful red flowers. Its botanical name is Butea monosperma.

The Soul of the Dinosaur

I

The train ran hurriedly over Rupa Bridge.

Maharaja[23] Rai Brajeswara Rai lifted the shutter's glass screen, condescendingly, and looked outside, carelessly, through the window. In the eastern sky, a reddish streak of light was coming out slowly, like an ornate bride emerging from her chamber and walking slovenly towards the marriage pedestal. The morning approached like a blushful lady slowly lifting her enshrouding veil of darkness.

Brajeswara Rai's head seemed heavier due to last night's overdose of whisky.

Yes . . . Rupa Bridge. Below the bridge, River Rupa's zigzag stream lied on the sand like an exhausted woman who had slept with her partner last night. Who was this sensuous and concupiscent woman? Madhavi? Mohini? Srimati? Anuradha?

Brajeswara lighted the extinguished cigar. Nothing really had changed in the last ten years. The same recognizable landscape on the very familiar banks of River

23   King

Rupa! The same old station of Rajkanchangarh right in front! Nothing had really changed.

A span of ten years was nothing. Brajeswara took off his woollen sleeping gown and threw it sloppily on the bed.

Returning to Rajkanchangarh on this wintry morning even after a gap of ten years made his drunken head fresh and rejuvenated. The train slowed down while whistling deafeningly during its final approach towards the old, dilapidated station-yard. From the platform a loud chorus of multiple voices rose; it was in fact a glory-slogan sung by the congregated public in the Maharaja's honour. Brajeswara listened with keen ears . . . "Victory to Maharaja Brajeswara Rai . . . Long live Maharaja Brajeswara Rai." His cruel and savage iron-face got slightly wrinkled with a thin ray of sepia-tainted smile that flickered only for a few countable moments, and vanished into the moist air like a tiny, little bird.

The train stopped inside the station-yard for a few minutes. Brajeswara peeped through its window and looked nonchalantly at the platform. After an enforced exodus for ten long years, he had today returned to Rajkanchangarh, with the lost grandeur of a dethroned king. The platform was heavily crowded to welcome him and no single space lied vacant and unoccupied inside its dreary and sepulchral premise. Of course, a lot had changed in these years. Rajkanchangarh had no more remained a kingdom; the kingship was gone and along with it was also gone royalty and its ostentatious grandeur.

The proliferating rust of growing age on Brajeswara's iron body was eminently visible . . .

He opened the door of the compartment with a condescending expression of disdain on his face.

Three servants quietly came inside. One of them quickly dressed him in his conventional regal attire; another held a water pot and a towel to him so that he would wash his face and then wipe it; another one brought the morning tea in a tray. Outside the compartment, the public went on chanting relentlessly 'Long Live Brajeswara Rai'; it went on repeatedly like the collective chanting of some divine mantra. His belongings were unloaded from another compartment. Lots of guns, many boxes, cameras etc.! Brajeswara slowly descended from the train's coupe onto the platform. It looked as if the tranquil morning sky trembled in the public's glory-slogan. Brajeswara's face was almost invisible from within the piles of dew-laden, marigold garlands.

He smoked form his pipe and asked someone: "How are you Mahapatra? Are these all Rajkanchangarh's people?"

Nilambara Mahapatra answered: "These are Rajkanchangarh's people, Your Excellency. Listening to the news of your arrival, they have accumulated here since dawn; these are the ones who have bedecked the gates with gorgeous designs and have placed festooned pots on the roadside for your grand welcome.

******

Another ten-year-old memory floated before Brajeswara's eyes like a momentary flash of an extended vision. It was the tale of a dark and sombre night in September, 1942. The British political agent Mitchell Sahib told him in a whiskey-drunken, drowsy voice: "Brajeswara

Rai! You have to leave Rajkanchangarh right now by the orders of the mighty British government. It's an exile of ten years for you."

Outside the Rajkanchangarh palace, the agitated mob stood lined with country-made rifles and dynamites in their hands; they wanted nothing else but the tyrant Brajeswara's blood. This Nilambara Mahapatra had that day clandestinely led Brajeswara to safety and had left him in the railway station. He was the most trusted lieutenant of this cruel and ruthless king. After Brajeswara's compulsive exile, Nilambara also spent three long years in prison for being the former's notorious accomplice in many of his atrocities on the public.

Mahapatra shouted at the mob: "Give way you rascals. Give way to the king."

A Roles Royse car arrived within moments and parked outside the gate with great difficulty. The accumulated mob was pushed away by Mahapatra and a few of his accomplices with virulence and disdain. Brajeswara promptly got into the car without glancing at the gathered people. Nilambara Mahapatra quickly climbed onto the driver's seat and started driving the vehicle.

Though Brajeswara's appearance had undergone multiple transformations over the years, the same regal cruelty persisted on his scraggy, emaciated body. The same bestiality sparkled on his pale, lacklustre forehead filled with clusters of dishevelled hair. His age-old heinousness glittered through the penetrative vision of his razor-sharp eyes.

Brajeswara told: "Drive fast Mahapatra! I should reach the fort in an hour and fifteen minutes." The fort was seventy miles away from the railway station; but the vehicle ran at a speed of only ten miles per hour due to the blockade caused by the assembled public.

Mahapatra increased the vehicle's speed a little and told: "Sir! It's really difficult to drive fast through the mob."

They would have just met with an accident. A person was hysterically rushing in, to garland the speeding vehicle's bonnet.

Brajeswara shouted at the mob: "Fools! Morons! Don't you know that obstructing the public road is a punishable offence?" Then he instructed Mahapatra to drive even faster.

But Mahapatra argued; "Sir! These rascals have come from long distances to honour you, Your Excellency."

Brajeswara left out a mouthful of smoke into the air through the car's open window and said: "One day this ignominious bunch of rascals came from long distances and accumulated here to drink my blood. Neither their love nor their enmity has value for me anymore. I cannot act before them with folded hands. You drive fast, Mahapatra. You drive fast."

The vehicle vanished with loud horns in the midst of a raising whirlwind of reddish dust.

II

In the sprawling garden of the Rajkanchangarh palace, Brajeswara loitered with a barrel-gun in his slender, scraggy hand.

In the blue sky flew innumerable flocks of cranes,

kites and sparrows filling its empty space with their loud and congregated twitters. Somewhere else, across the sky flew another flock of teal-ducks, like a garland of jasmines gliding aimlessly on its long-stretching, bluish floor. Brajeswara aimed at them and fired from his gun; some of the birds fell on the ground being hit by his bullets. A feeling of extreme contentment bloomed on his stupendously glazing iron-face. A gardener ran to search for the dead and the injured birds.

Another flock of birds came flying with loud twitters in the sky.

Their thirst for life was not quenched at the Caspian Sea. Its chilling winter propelled them towards the equatorial areas for the life-giving warmth that the latter offered. On their wings there was the mysterious allure of distances; in their throats, there was the mellifluous song of life. . . Brajeswara aimed at them once again and fired from his barrel gun. Some till ducks dipped through the air fluttering their wounded wings and then, fell on the ground. From their kaleidoscopic wings dripped tiny, delicate drops of blood onto the soil whose crispy sand was drenched in red.

Brajeswara lifted one bird in his hand in condescending cruelty. Death was slowly engulfing the bird like a baneful spell of sorcery cast on it by an invisible and devilish sorcerer. Brajeswara threw the bird on the ground without the slightest feeling of remorse or mercy. Of course, it was another matter that these days he no more enjoyed such rampant wastage of energy in gunning down birds. There was no excitement in these heartless killings anymore. He slovenly strolled back towards the palace placing the rusted barrel gun on his shoulder.

The soporific white shade of the palace danced on the adjacent pond's crystal-clear water like an adroit classical dancer. Brajeswara was startled by the restless twitter of a bird from within a tranquil cypress bush. The palace looked still, quiet and tranquilized, bereft of anybody's pulsating presence around. An atrocious and meaningless futility reigned over the whole ambience that had turned uncharacteristically sterile and comatose. Everywhere there was the empty profusion lifelessness. Brajeswara leisurely walked towards the palace with a downcast head.

In the front portico, some people were waiting fortuitously to greet him. At the news of his arrival at Rajkanchangarh after so many years, large contingents of citizens from his lost kingdom flew from distances every day to meet their king. The kingdom was lost; the kingship was gone; yet, their love, loyalty and allegiance for the dethroned king still lingered in their subconscious—firm and unshaken like a sacramental bond. Looking at Brajeswara, they paid him obeisance by prostrating before him. Brajeswara did not pay any heed. He took off his gun from his shoulder, handed it over to a servant and quietly went inside the palace.

Inside, he asked Mahapatra: "Why has this senseless bunch of people assembled here? What do they need? Drive them away."

Mahapatra said: "Your Excellency! The way time is changing, it's both beneficial and profitable to keep them in hand. Shall it be appropriate to drive these rascals away when they have come from distances with so much of love and adoration for you?"

Brajeswara answered in a slightly agitated voice: "Yes! Times have changed. But I have not. Neither do I have any desire to change."

Mahapatra left.

Everywhere there was the cruel, pitiless laughter of atrocious destiny! And also the meaningless profusion of regal opulence . . . The multicoloured rose garden was clearly visible through the open window. It seemed to Brajeswara as if his life was nothing but an attractive lady's beautiful and polished marble statue. She could be felt, but could not be enjoyed; she could be drunk; but that won't quench his thirst. Inside the shining and colourful ambience of the palace, Brajeswara felt terribly alone, distraught and incapacitated. His violent and irrepressible desire for flesh burnt into flames inside his desiccated veins and then was extinguished in a moment.

Brajeswara called: "Who is there?"

A servant rushed in and stood before him with a downcast head and waited for an order. Brajeswara ordered: "Whisky and Soda."

They were brought immediately. He sipped some whiskey from the glass and placed it on the nearby table.

Mahapatra came in and told: "Your Excellency! Damodar Raiguru has come to meet you".

Brajeswara asked: "Which Damodar Raiguru?"

Mahapatra told: "The same Damodar Raiguru of Ranidaha who had girdled the palace with armed rebels in the blinding depths of the night during the citizens' revolt. Let me send him back by bluntly telling him that you cannot meet him."

Brajeswara said: "No! Send him straight to me, Mahapatra. Send him straight to me."

After some time came Damodar Raiguru, a fairly

aged man with slackened skin and sunken eyes. The hair on his head flew like cornstalk in the wind. He had been a participant in many revolutions against the British government and had been imprisoned many a times. The grievous torture that he received in jail was still visible on his face as a clear and inerasable imprint. Damodar paid regards to Brajeswara with a bow.

Brajeswara asked: "What new demands do you have Raiguru? I have fulfilled all your demands."

Raiguru smiled gently and said: "What demand, Your Excellency? Nothing! Things are going from bad to worse here, in Rajkanchangarh."

Brajeswara told: "That is quite ok. You are destined either for the good or for the bad. God almighty has written nothing more on your forehead."

Raiguru asked: "Means?"

Brajeswara lighted his pipe with a characteristic display of heedlessness and said: "The meaning is very simple Raiguru. To exploit is the nature of man. He created the nation to protect the weak from exploitation by the strong. But the nation became more atrocious and exploitative than the man himself. Tell me who had thought of it?"

Raiguru asked: "Then why did we put an end to monarchy?"

Brajeswara left a mouthful of smoke from his pipe and answered: "There was a huge flaw in monarchy, Raiguru. I was exploiting and torturing the citizens without their consent; but democracy does the same with their consent. For instance, in monarchy, I could crack your head without taking your permission; but in democracy, I can do the same with your kind permission." After uttering these words, Brajeswara started laughing loudly.

Raiguru said: "Even I have started believing in exploitation, Your Excellency. Man does not rely on anything else other than exploitation. The human civilization, society, culture, and religion—everything is built on the foundation of fear. As long as there is exploitation, the human society shall continue to remain safe and secure. If there is no fear of exploitation, then man cannot be bonded in the incarcerations of the society."

Brajeswara left into his room. He did not want to further engage in such futile discussions.

III

It was evening.

Brajeswara stood near his rest room's window and looked at the moon-blanched garden sprawling outside like a colourful carpet spread out on a ragged and pebbly landscape. From within the thick foliage of the Eucalyptus and casuarinas trees, the full-blown moon rose slowly like the hallucinatory image of an unknown prince in the dreamy eyes of a despondent princess. Brajeswara had finished off all the whiskey from his glass in one, gigantic gulp. Coming back from the window, he sat languidly on a decorated sofa while looking vacuously at a kaleidoscopic chandelier that dangled from the roof like a gaudy fragment of memory. It dangled like a piece of reminiscence from his old, lecherous and despotic days. The severed heads of some hunted down tigers hanged on his wall as taxidermy. A hunger brimmed on their huge, ravenous tongues that looked awfully detestable and terrifying. The ageless hunger for flesh persisted on them even after the tigers' death while a ghostlike silence reigned over the dingy room's murky atmosphere. Inside, the dim electric bulb emitted clusters of unrecognizable, thin rays.

Brajeswara pressed the electric switch of the calling-bell. Within some time, Nilambara Mahapatra came in with hastened steps. Brajeswara lighted his pipe and said: "The evening looks beautiful and sensuous, Mahapatra."

Mahapatra said: "Yes, Your Excellency! It looks really beautiful."

Brajeswara left a mouthful of smoke from his pipe and told: "But Mahapatra! The beauty is not to be enjoyed alone. Have you arranged for something? I mean a delicate, fleshy virgin—untouched, uninitiated . . ."

Mahapatra answered with the tone of an apologist: "Sir, gone are those days when we could drag anybody to your feet with force or money. The time has grown difficult."

Brajeswara said: "What is the problem? First there was the fear of the ruler. We could confiscate anything from anybody by the sheer display of power and might. Can we not do the same now?

Mahapatra answered with a clear and unambiguous gesture of disapproval: "I don't believe so, Your Excellency. It cannot be done now."

Brajeswara took another peg of whiskey and drank it silently. Then he lifted the emptied glass before his eyes for a few seconds and told while surveying something mysterious inside it: "I have heard Mahapatra, you have a rare piece of diamond inside your own house. Why should you look for it outside?"

Nilambara Mahapatra's eyes lit up like two burning pieces of coal inside a mine. His expressions became harder, complicated and unexpectedly rebellious. He said in an enraged and unapologetic voice: "I am indebted to you for life, Your Excellency. But I have not eaten up my conscience. No father in this world can accept such a dirty and detestable proposal. I cannot believe that you can be so outrageously savage and unabashed."

Mahapatra prepared to leave while thumping his feet violently on the ground. Brajeswara called form behind: "Listen Mahapatra."

Mahapatra stopped like a statue in a slavish response to Brajeswara's inviolable orders. Brajeswara kept loitering with a few silent steps inside the room and told: "You have violated your conscience many a times in the past to maintain your deathless allegiance to me, Mahapatra. And you know that quite well. Don't you remember how many hundreds of times you have compelled hapless fathers to send their daughters to me?"

Mahapatra said with folded hands and in a softened voice: "Forgive me, Your Excellency. I cannot do it anymore. It's my own daughter."

Brajeswara threw a bunch of keys at Mahapatra and said: "Open that iron safe."

Nilambara Mahapatra obliged like a robot. It was full of sparkling gold jewelleries. His eyes lit up at their blinding resplendence.

Brajeswara said: "The royal mother had preserved

them all for the royalty's future queen. You know Mahapatra! I love to confiscate things rather than obtaining them as gifts or by soliciting them like a beggar. And nobody knows it better than you. But rest assured that no single lady has worn these ornaments even once. If you wish, your beautiful daughter can wear them."

Mahapatra kept staring at Brajeswara unblinkingly like a hypnotized man. Brajeswara told: "I shall decorate her in my own hands as per her wishes."

Mahapatra sat on a couch like a dumb and immovable stone-effigy.

Brajeswara told: "I am waiting. Send her quickly."

IV

The night had deepened into an immense and inexplicable quietude.

Outside, the full-moon-night's moon descended down the horizon like a lost, celestial traveller. The palace-garden slowly got enshrouded by a thick cover of darkness.

Brajeswara poured the last few pegs of whiskey into the glass and told: "Sundari! You have a beautiful name. There is no exaggeration in it; it's easy and simple and truly justifies your elegant, fine-spun and supple body's unmatchable delicacy and splendour. You are truly beautiful, Sundari. You are truly beautiful."

Sundari was Nilambara Mahapatra's daughter. Brajeswara had heard it right. She was incomparably attractive and sensuous.

She stood near Brajeswara with a downcast head

that was half-buried in her breasts. She trembled like an injured deer hit by a hunter's arrow. She did not have the courage to look at the lecherous Brajeswara's ruthless, drunken face.

Breaking the silence, Brajeswara told: "Why don't you come closer, Sundari? Why do you stand there alone?"

Sundari didn't say anything and stood mum with her head buried in her breasts.

Brajeswara advanced towards her and lifted her veil while holding her exquisite chin in his right hand. He could readily spot a dark mole.

Brajeswara told in a seductive tone: "Sundari! This mole looks gorgeous and provocative like a bride's secret desire."

Sundari kept quiet like a dumb cow.

Brajeswara undressed her in both his hands. She stood naked before him, like the shy, bashful moonlit night bereft of the cover of darkness. Her pliant breasts were thoroughly uncovered. Her thick, delicate thighs looked like being carved in polished marble by an adroit artisan by sheer diligence.

Brajeswara told: "It's a beautiful symmetry, Sundari. It's a beautiful symmetry."

Sundari blushed and covered her face with her hands.

Brajeswara removed the remaining dresses from her body.

While resisting, Sundari's hand inadvertently hit the dark mole on her chin. The mole got partly erased and ran haphazardly along her softened cheek like a shady, unclear line. She had in fact drawn it in collyrium to make her face look more appealing, winsome and seductive.

Brajeswara said: "Your mole is erased now, Sundari. What was the need for you to paint your rosy cheek with a brush?"

Thoroughly denuded, Sundari sat on the sofa with her face covered by her hands. She had mixed feelings of shame, fear and apprehensions. She looked like a charming stone-carved effigy sculpted by an adroit artisan.

Brajeswara kept loitering silently inside his room with his arms folded against his chest. The thudding sound of his shoes engulfed Sundari's faint and almost inaudible heartbeat like a ravenous beast.

Finally, he stopped near her and asked: "Can you tell Sundari which is more beautiful? The moonlit night or the enticing nudity of your body?

Sundari kept looking at him dumbfounded, speechless.

Brajeswara opened the iron safe in his own hands and said: "These are all yours, Sundari. You take whatever you like. Your price! I am leaving. You can bolt the door from inside."

Brajeswara left the room and started walking through the night without direction. Undressed, Sundari kept watching him dissolve in the moonlight like a faint and unrecognizable shadow. Brajeswara kept walking and walking across time's endless trajectories, into the dark and circuitous depths of History. He was turning into a gigantic animal, a quadruped with huge, protruding canines, and sharpened claws and a prolonging, thorny tail. He kept sliding into the depths of the night and into the dark, dungeon of cruel time. He was a dinosaur.

*****

Srikrishna's Last Laugh

That day it seemed as if the sun had stopped his chariot for a moment to witness the concluding scene of *Mahabharata* in Indraprastha.

After the end of *Mahabharata*, Kurukhsetra's abandoned battlefield was filled with the dispersed debris of many ornamented chariots and with the mutilated bodies of millions of Kaurava soldiers scattered all around. Their distressed wives led by late Duryodhana's wife Bhanumati frantically ran through the field looking for their loved ones from amongst the gigantic and petrifying mounds of bodies. Their heartrending screams submerged and obfuscated the loathsome and terrifying shouts of bloodthirsty dogs, jackals and the vultures.

Death had engulfed every little commotion in Kurukshetra. Every sound including that of the horses and the tuskers had become tranquilized under its pervasive and marauding spell. The battlefield was infested with swarming army of wild dogs and jackals whereas above in the stultifying sky, reeled like dark shades the flesh-loving kites in large flocks.

Dhrutarastra's palace in Indraprastha had turned

disquieted and people-less. At times Sanjaya and Bidura were found to be loitering helter-skelter inside the tranquil room with plaintive moods. The slow sound of their footsteps made the overall climate of the palace grave, gloomy and pestilential. Dhrutarastra's pitiful sighs and Gandhari's heartrending cries were getting heavier.

Dhrutarastra was blind from birth. He had lost all his hundred sons, his friends and lieutenants including Karna, Drona, Bhurisraba etc. in Kurukhsetra's battlefield. His buoyant aspirations to see them for the last time ricocheted from the four walls of his room and were sealed in its comatose, cadaverous silence, like incarcerated birds in a cage. But Gandhari thought of throwing away her eye-cover and seeing her son's bodies for the first and the last time; but her proscriptive and irrevocable vow during her marriage to Dhrutarastra, as a devoted wife, made it impossible for her. As a sanctified and ceremonious wife, she could not have crossed over the ethical circumscriptions laid down by herself. But if she had not vowed that day, today she would have easily thrown away her eye-covers to see those bodies.

Gandhari was the mother of one hundred sons— Duryodhana, Duhsasana, Durjaya, Duranta, Durgama, Durtara, Durbalaka . . . ; she was the glory of Somabansa[24]. The sons who slept only on the gorgeous, comfortable cushions on their cots, now slept on their murky deathbeds in Kurukhsetra's muddy, pestiferous battlefield.

The egregious rampage of dogs, jackals and kites on their bodies created a ghastly scene all around.

Gandhari emitted a sharp cry of pain when she

---

24   -The glorious clan into which Gandhari and the Kauravas belonged.

heard the intimidating sound of a flock of kites swooping feverishly on the abandoned bodies.

She lifted both her arms into the air and cried: "Bidura, Sanjaya . . ."

Her pitiful cry echoed for some time inside the hall and then was engulfed by the ghostly silence of the pathetically depopulated Kaurava palace.

*****

Blind Dhrutarastra lifted his two arms into the air with a futile display of inconsequential vainglory and boasted before Bidura: "Don't forget Bidura! Even today I have the power to smash the Kaurava-killers—these Pandavas—to dust, in my two arms."

Dhrutarastra shouted like a lion sitting on the dazzling but disenfranchised Kaurava throne. The muscles on his wrinkled face stiffened obdurately. His eyes sparkled like a dead volcano sprung to life.

Bidura told in a cool and composed voice: "Your Excellency, great king! All the Dhrutarastras are eternally blind. The power and vainglory of the throne has perennially eclipsed and obfuscated their vision. Eyes are not the only vision, king. Where was your vision when the Kauravas wanted to treacherously finish off the Pandavas in the lac- house? Where was your vision when the five sons of Draupadi were slaughtered, bestially, in sleep? Where was your vision when Draupadi was denuded and puckishly humiliated in the fully occupied Kaurava palace before everybody? Where was your vision when Duryodhana boasted, while vaingloriously thumping his chest, before Srikrishna's convoy that he would not give the Pandavas even a pinch of soil without war? If you had been jurisprudent and righteous as a king during those conflicted times, today you would not have confronted such unwelcome and dire consequences, my king. That is why I keep reiterating that it is not just you, but it is all the Dhrutarastras who are perennially blinded."

Dhrutarastra answered; "But I had never thought, even in my wildest fancy, that the great warriors like Bhisma, Karna and Drona etc. will be so easily defeated and decimated by this impoverished and destitute bunch of Pandavas."

Bidura answered: "That is why I keep telling that all the Dhrutarastras are perennially blinded. The demands for justice by the exploited, however weak and vulnerable they may be, can never be trampled and suppressed by your oceanic and deleterious Kaurava army. History shall always derogate and ridicule many Indraprasthas, many Hastinapuras and many Barunabantas for their blatant and meaningless exhibition of ineffectual vainglory. The great King! The peace and sovereignty of 'Bharata'[25] shall be achieved not through the callous humiliation of the destitute, rather through uplifting them with a sagacious display of kindness and fellow-feeling."

Listening to Bidura's sermonic admonitions, Dhrutarastra started shouting in a way as if the sky would tumble on Earth with an uproarious bang. Lambasting Bidura with a grave and thunderous voice, Dhrutarastra said: "Bidura! You are the slave of the Kauravas. You have grown up on the food and kindness provided to you by your so-called callous and vainglorious Kauravas. Today, when they are in great distress, you are giving them the appropriate gift with your unkind and hurtful words.

25   -The ancient name of India.

There is not even a single word of comfort and solace in your voice for the Kauravas."

Bidura responded with an unperturbed voice: "Great King! Truth however bitter, tough and unpleasant it may be has to be confronted one day."

Dhrutarastra shouted again: "But for a small and insignificant territory, the whole Kaurava race will be demolished. Do you agree to it, Bidura?" How would I forget Bidura? The flagrant, lighted candles of the Somabansa are getting extinguished one by one. Like my own blindness, the future of my race looks bleak, inconsequential and dismal."

Bidura responded in a cool and unruffled voice; "The great king! Accept this destiny as a consequence of your relentless and grievous wrongdoings. You will get peace. You have destroyed your own race by turning blind eyes to their prolonged and persistent injustices and misdeeds. Pandavas are only a small, negligible race. Don't harm them any more out of your injudicious anger and vengeance."

During that time, the grieving Gandhari came rushing in like a mad woman with her eyes blindfolded and said: "Great king! One day I had wilfully put these covers on my eyes as an inviolable vow, as a token of sympathy and honour for your accursed blindness. Liberate me from my oath today great king. I am the mother of your one hundred sons. I have never seen them in my eyes when they were alive. Let me see them today when they are dead. Let my grieving eyes get some conciliation and solace."

Gandhari wanted to tear off her eye-cover with a feeling of an unstoppable and undeletable urgency to see her dead sons' bodies, splayed right in her front. In the process, she inadvertently scratched her face with her fingernails and started bleeding copiously from the wound. The blood oozing from her injured face made her look terribly ugly, mephitic and gruesome.

Gandhari shrieked again in an awfully broken voice: "Great king! I have always remained blindfolded because of you despite having my healthy vision intact. Today, take off my eye-covers for once great king and let me see my dead sons."

Listening to Gandhari's requests, Dhrutarastra's face became pale and lacklustre like a piece of dark, febrile cloud. Gandhari did not know (But Dhrutarastra knew) that below that superfluous cover, there were not just her dormant eyes, but were two giant, hibernating volcanoes. Once she opened them, even Dhrutarastra would burn to a shapeless pile of ashes within a few moments.

Bidura tried to comfort Gandhari and told: "Try to control your grief great lady. Who tells you do not have sons anymore? Under the protection of the Pandava king Yudhisthira, your son Durdasa is still alive." Moreover, the five Pandavas love and adore you like their own mother."

Gandhari started shouting again: "I know great king! This eye-cover shall never come out. Right from the beginning till the end, Gandhari's life will only be about noxious darkness and irremediable grief and nothing else."

Gandhari had come floating towards Dhrutarastra like a dry, desiccated, windblown leaf; and went back like the same blown away in a passing, twirling whirlwind.

*****

The festooned chariot was ready to glide towards a preordained destination, carrying the war-triumphant Dharmaraja Yudhisthira on its cushioned recliner. In the nick of time, Srikrishna approached him from an opposite direction and asked: "On the eve of your propitious coronation as Hastinapura's celebrated and illustrious king, where are you going alone Dharmaraja[26]?

Yudhisthira said; "Mother Gandhari has summoned me. I am going to meet her."

Srikrishna responded peevishly: "I have also not met mother Gandhari for quite some time now. Then let's go together. I shall drive your chariot."

Yudhisthira was taken aback by Srikrishna's abrupt and unsolicited propositions and asked: "What is this new mystery, Mayadhara[27]?"

Srikrishna sprung onto the charioteer's seat and responded in his archetypal, alchemistic voice: "Do you forget Dharmaraja I am the one who had led this once blood-stained chariot to victory through Mahabharata's sanguinary battlefront. Are you doubting me, Yudhisthira?"

Embarrassed and shame-faced, Yudhisthira kept mum.

Srikrishna had always remained a mysterious character like this.

*****

Gandhari roamed with Sanjaya through the mass grave of Kurukshetra's battlefront while madly scrambling

---

26   Yudhisthira was famously called 'Dharmaraja' for being the pro-
     tector of 'dharma' or righteousness.
27   Krishna was called 'Mayadhara' for being an expert in the art of
     creating 'maya' or illusion.

for her one hundred sons from amongst the massive and horrendous pile of blood-stained bodies. In the diminishing lights of the dusk, Sanjaya led her through the ravenous crowd of dogs, jackals and kites into the midst of these bodies scattered all around like dried and crumpled leaves strewn putridly over a storm-ravaged landscape.

Sanjaya told: "Great lady! Look how the legendary Bhisma lies out there on the soil in the deepest slumber of his life. Look at the hermetic, calm repose on his face." Gandhari said: "I know Sanjaya! He has relinquished his life in his own volition. Otherwise the Pandavas were nothing before his world-beating might."

Sanjaya said: "And here lies the war-hero Somadatta, smashed under a chariot-wheel and there lies the great Bhurishraba wounded to death by the mad tusker's internecine tusks. Great lady! Here lies the war-hero Karna, barged by the arrows of archer Arjuna. On the split and fractured crown on his head is stuck the last ray of the setting sun, like the deific blessing of the father on his son's head. With that ray's sparkling luminosity, Karna's face still glows with the resplendence of a hundred blooming lotuses in a sun-bathed, shimmering pond."

Gandhari held Karna's body in her breasts in a tight, passionate embrace and said in a choked voice: "Come boy! You have been deprived of a mother's affection all your life—

you, the greatest Pandava. Come to me. Let me embrace you. You, the protector of Duryodhana's arrogance! I cannot see you lying here in this wretched condition on this muddy and abandoned battlefield. But O almighty! O omnipotent! O creator! Is there no retribution for those who have defied the Khsatriya[28] principles and killed Karna through treachery?"

After moving some distance, Sanjaya told: "Great lady! Here lies Duhsasana deflated on the soil, his thighs smashed by Bhima's gigantic mace. It was Bhima's vow to avenge his obscene behaviour towards Draupadi's denuded thighs in the crammed Kaurava court. His pearl-decorated necklace still dazzles on his wide chest, like the sparkle of lightening across the jumble of blue clouds. Let's go great lady! This is the eternal game of life and death. Everybody is entitled to his deeds."

A vexatious outburst of a sharp cry of pain filled Gandhari's voice and she told: "Remove my eye-cover once Sanjaya. This is the son whom I have never seen in my life. At least let me see his body and pacify my eyes."

A little away from Gandhari, Srikrishna curtailed the speed of his chariot. Yudhisthira asked in a fretful voice: "Why did you decelerate the chariot's speed, Narayana[29]?"

Srikrishna answered with a gentle but carousing smile: "We should not go with the arrogance of victory to someone who suffers from unbearable pain and agony. In addition, Gandhari is like your mother."

Yudhisthira got down from the chariot like a wrongdoer and said: "You are absolutely right Narayana. I should go to grief-stricken mother Gandhari on bare foot."

Yudhisthira was nonchalantly walking towards Gandhari sitting and bewailing rambunctiously near

---

28   -It refers to the race of warriors. They are expected to fight the battles on the basis of certain heroic principles, not through deception.

29   -Another name for Srikrishna.

Duryodhana's slain body when Srikrishna hastily pulled him back by one arm and said: "Do you know Yudhisthira why Gandhari has summoned you?"

Yudhisthira said: No! I do not know that."

Srikrishna smiled gently again and said: "Gandhari wants you to remove her eye-cover so that she can see the bodies of her sons from amongst the pile in Kurukshetra's crematory ground."

Yudhisthira told: "Is it a very difficult thing to do?" I shall tear off her eye-cover this moment."

Srikrishna smiled astutely and told: "But Yudhisthira! How do you forget that the mother of one hundred sons Gandhari is today sonless because of you Pandavas?" In her comprehension, the whole of the Kaurava race has been demolished because of your lofty aspirations for the throne."

Yudhisthira told in a helpless voice: "I don't know whether she knows it or not; but, you know it all great God."

Srikrishna answered: "After you remove Gandhari's eye-cover, she would see her son Duryodhana's body first and then will she not be filled with a feeling of anger and vengeance instead of that of love and compassion?"

Yudhisthira asked in a stupefied voice: "That is true Krishna. But when mother Gandhari has called me to do the job, what should I do?"

Srikrishna told: "All the hundred sons of Gandhari might have perished; but her son Durdasa is still alive. Gandhari's anger can be pacified when she sees her son Durdasa."

Gandhari could hear Yudhisthira's voice from a distance when the former conversed with Srikrishna and she asked Sanjaya: "Sanjaya! Is this not Yudhisthira's voice that I hear?"

Sanjaya said: "Srikrishna and all the Pandava brothers have arrived to pay obeisance to you, mother."

Exalted, Gandhari lifted two of her arms in the air to embrace Yudhisthira and told: "Come, Yudhisthira, come! The living embodiment of compassion, the Pandava leader! Today you are also the Kaurava leader. I am the sinner; I have received the consequences of my misdeeds in the past. Please remove my opaque eye-cover once, son. I have never seen my hundred sons when they were alive; let me see them in their death for the last time and let me pacify my craving eyes."

Listening to Gandhari's pitiful words, Yudhisthira was going to remove her eye-cover; but Srikrishna stopped him from behind by holding one of his arms. Then he turned towards Gandhari's only surviving son Durdasa and said: "Durdasa! You go and remove your mother's eye-cover. The mother who has lost almost all her sons will at least get some consolation to see her only surviving son."

There was a mysterious smile in Srikrishna's lips.

Yudhisthira told Durdasa: "Do what says Srikrishna."

Durdasa wilfully obliged Yudhisthira's orders and expeditiously removed Gandhari's eye-cover.

The moment it was removed, the conflagrant flames of infuriation and vengeance flung outside from within the dark and infernal pits of her eyes like an impetuous volcanic eruption. In those apocalyptic flames, Durdasa turned into an amorphous pile of ashes within no time and collapsed on Duryodhana's body.

Yudhisthira shouted; "What did you do you foxy and guileful Srikrishna? Durdasa was most loyal to me."

Srikrishna told in a contorted voice "Keep quiet you moron. If Durdasa did not burn into ashes in the flames of Gandhari's eyes, how would you be coroneted tomorrow as Hastinapura's king? This is politics . . . Such sacrifices of these loyal and allegiant Durdasas in the blazing furnace of politics is a routine thing. You should not be so aghast by such a small and negligible incident, Yudhisthira."

Sanjaya told in an abject voice, as if struck by a lightening: "What did you do great lady? You destroyed in your own hand the last insignia of the Kaurava race, Durdasa."

Srikrishna feigned compassion and said: "Mother! Who says you are sonless? Who are the Kauravas and who are the Pandavas? They are all your sons. Now accept the Pandavas as your sons."

Another mysterious smile floated on his face.

Gandhari looked down at the mango-bud-like fallen body of Durdasa at her feet and laughed boisterously in a frenzied manner and said: "I have understood everything Srikrishna! I have understood your foxy manoeuvres. But mark my words you congenital crook. You can never retain the throne by dint of your Sudarshan wheel's power. Everything shall be burnt by a grieving mother's curses. Even you won't be spared Srikrishna. Like the Somabansa, the Yadubansa[30] shall one day perish through internecine

---

30   -Lord Srikrishna's clan.

conflicts. Even your favourite son Pradyumna won't be spared. This is my curse, the curse of a mother who has lost her one hundred sons in the battlefield. My curse won't go in vain. Remember that Srikrishna. Remember that."

Crying inconsolably, Gandhari collapsed on the ashes of Durdasa.

There was another mysterious smile on Srikrishna's face which however was engulfed by the approaching darkness.

In the marooned sky above the Indraprastha mountain range, the blazing sun was also preparing to set in the west.

*****

Father and Son

I

At the top of the hill, there was a small prison house; it had a tiny hole through which the morning sunlight flooded in and lightened its enormous, sprawling dark space. The din and bustle of the citizenry was clearly audible from the high way meandering through the curvy patterns of the hill like a sliding serpent.

Through the hole, the prisoner threw a hungry and haggard glance at the immense profusion of light spreading outside like a blissful enigma. It was the morning's quiet and resplendent ray of light, just like the holy blessing of Lord Buddha.

Being old and exposed to relentless atrocities, the prisoner looked hungry, scraggy and emaciated like a ghost dangling imperceptibly in the air. The wide chest that he once possessed and flaunted before the world with limitless valour and vainglory was now covered with grubbed masses of pale, gray-white hairs. His dazzling skin had slackened like a wrinkled piece of cloth.

The prisoner was the Magadha king Bimbisara dethroned and imprisoned by his son Ajatasatru who had usurped his throne through a clandestine coup.

On Ajatasatru's inviolable orders, he had been imprisoned here under this living tomb.

The former had vowed to kill him—to kill him by hunger.

In enormous exhaustion and deep depression, Bimbisara's two sunken eyelids closed down again and his limbs were getting paralysed in extreme hunger. He dragged his thirsty tongue over his desiccated lips and screamed in a choked voice—a scream that reverberated inside the prison house like the bloodcurdling roar of a haunted-down lion.

This beautiful and monumental palace was once built in his order. Today in its dark, grimy and secluded chamber and away from his incredibly loyal citizens, he felt in every moment the excruciating pangs of death. These were perhaps the retributions for his previous birth's misdeeds—he kept thinking.

A huge and uncontrollable fire once broke out in his earlier capital Kusagranagara. Almost the whole of the city was charred into scattered piles of debris. Bimbisara ordered that the person whose house shall catch fire shall be irrevocably exiled into deep and dense forests. But strange and inexplicable was the law of Nature. His own palace once caught fire and following a principle laid down by himself, the king accepted self-imposed exile in 'Seetalabana'.

The great king was overawed by the exquisite scenic beauty of this place situated on the banks of river 'Sarpini' and surrounded by splendid mountains like 'Bipulagiri,' 'Baibharagiri' and 'Grudhrakuta.' By his inviolable orders, here was built the new and spectacular capital city of Magadha—Rajagruha.

With great difficulty, Bimbisara lifted his exhausted, comatose pair of eyes to have a last, piteous look at Rajagruha—the eyes that had turned into a pair of immovable stones—lifeless and visionless.

That day when Ajatasatru imprisoned his father Bimbisara, the former's grief-stricken, shrivelled-haired and tearful mother pleaded for mercy before her son:

"Son Ajatasatru."

Ajatasatru answered in a taunting voice riddled with an ignominious sense of ridicule: "Give orders Your Excellency, the princess of Kashi[31]".

"Is it such a shameful thing for you to call me mother, son?" Said the mother in a heartbroken voice.

"Son! Ha-Ha-Ha! Ajatasatru laughed boisterously and then said in a cruel and gravelly voice: "I do not shy away from calling you my mother. But can you please explain to me what will be the son's reply to a mother who once contemplated to slaughter him for the fear of a rumoured patricide that he was supposed to commit after growing up?"

Koshala Devi answered in a shivering tone: "I have told you hundreds of times son that this is nothing but a rumour that had spread through the city like a whirlwind."

Ajatasatru said: "There is no smoke without fire,

---

31   -Ajatasatru's mother Koshala Devi was the princess of the king-
        dom of Kashi.

princess of Kashi. But why is this unnecessary discussion? I am ready to accept all your pleas and requests except the one pertaining to Bimbisara's unconditional release."

Koshala Devi wiped away her tears in her saree and told: "Ok fine! If your coronation shall be at the expense of your father's blood, then who can resist it, my son? But I have only one solicitation, king. Bimbisara never appreciated any dish except the one prepared by me. Today I want to serve him food in the prison in my own hands. Please do not deny me this small pleasure of mine."

Ajatasatru said with a voice of reassurance: "Ok! I grant your request, princess of Kashi. I grant your request."

But after Koshala Devi departed, he ordered his prison guard Chanda: "The prisoner must not touch even a grain of food served to him by Koshala Devi."

******

Almost empty was the smudgy water pot. Bimbisara lifted it with his violently shaking hands and tried to touch it with his lips. It fell from his wobbly hands and broke into splinters splayed on the ground. The morning sun had soared high up into the sky like a bright-winged eagle. The thin and slanted ray of light that had encroached into the chamber through a fissure had also disappeared. In the dark, grimy and foul-smelling prison house reigned nothing but the brooding, hellish atmosphere of death.

Hunger no more tortured Bimbisara. What remained were only an unquenched thirst and an agonizing sense of aloofness. "Now, I shall be liberated from that also"—thought the king. "Then it will only be a profound and unfathomable emptiness all around—like Buddha's meditation. The eyelids will be still and quiescent forever."

Bimbisara kept on murmuring these grievous words to himself while calmly accepting the vagaries of his destiny with saintly stoicism. It was a few moments of dull and monotonous silence thereafter and then, a murderous circle of emptiness closed down on him whispering in his ears the cruel message of death. But suddenly in his blurring vision, floated the statute of the meditating Buddha spread out against the vast expanses of the sky like a blooming lotus in a distant waterway. The peace and tranquillity in his half-closed eyes were brimful and abundant.

Due to excessive thirst, Bimbisara's tongue and lips had started bleeding with tiny droplets of dark, red blood. They quenched his thirst to an extent. In a choked voice, he shouted like a wounded animal.

In his diminishing vision, Bimbisara saw floating on the firmament of the sky the gorgeous Saptaparni ravine of the Grudhrakuta Mountain. One day he was perplexed by the news that the Sakya dynasty's prince Gautama had become a monk and was meditating in these tranquil and godforsaken ravines. It was a dusky evening with a cloudless sky when Bimbisara, flanked by large contingents of his royal officials, went to meet Gautama Buddha in Grudhrakuta. By that time, the latter was delivering sermons to some of his disciples in Saptaparni. In a garden on the mountain's foothill, the female peacocks enjoyed the dance of their male counterparts and kissed them through their beaks in an ecstasy of love and mutual adoration. In the nearby grassland, innumerable deer roamed with unbounded joy and excitement brimming uncontrollably through their dilate eyes. At a distance, a female deer looked at its own reflection in a pond's crystal-clear water and was lost in the secret appreciation of her own beauty.

Buddha was deeply immersed in his meditation; his limbs emanated resplendent, divine lights while a gigantic halo circled the rear of his head; the halo spread glittering, stellar rays all around. The calm repose of the dusk had precipitated in his half-closed eyes while his half-opened palms emanated heavenly blessings for tormented mankind. Bimbisara asked in a soothing, temperate voice: "What grief brings you to this deep meditation, prince?"

Gautama smiled gently and answered: "No grief drives me here, Your Excellency! In fàct, I am in search for its cause and its remedy."

Bimbisara laughed loudly and said: "The remedy is very simple, prince. But how would you get it in these deserted ravines of Saptaparni? Come then to the celebration hall of Rajagruha. You will get all your answers in the colourful wine frothing inside golden glasses and in the lascivious eyes of Magadha's voluptuous whores that shall be at your service."

Bimbisara laughed loudly again in luxuriant ecstasy. Gautama's two half-closed eyelids got heavier like the evening's approaching darkness.

After a few moments' silence, Gautama spoke: "The remedy of this thirst is not in the consummation of desire, king. It lies in its complete relinquishment."

Ah! The thirst was tearing apart Bimbisara's windpipe. The deathlike silence of the prison house's closed compartment echoed with those words of Buddha that ultimate happiness lies not in the fulfilment of desire, but in its complete annihilation. The Magadha whores danced no more; their dyed feet had become iron-chained; the pillaging gloom of death had filled their collyriumridden eyes. In the brimming golden pots, there no more danced the spilling out bubbles of wine, rather danced the gruesome and murderous foams of venom.

"Whose anklet's symphony do I hear? Koshala Devi? The queen?" Bimbisara asked himself vaguely imagining her presence around.

The prison-guards were changing. The jingling sound of their iron armours was faintly heard in the murky chambers of the prison house. In unbearable thirst, Bimbisara bit one of his arms like an injured wild animal.

II

Through the window, Ajatasatru kept staring at the spreading out and mist-enshrouded mountain ranges outside; there was no blink in his eyes. A few white and greyish clouds kept vacillating over the mountains like celestial travellers. Sporadic flocks of homeward cranes kept plunging into the horizon with their wings set ablaze with the setting sun's crimson light. On the cot was sleeping like a dead and waterless river Ajatasatru's pregnant wife Bajra, battling with unbearable labour pain. From the pigeon sty, many pigeons flew away into the sky and then, came back making large, disturbing sounds with their fluttering wings. Seeing a few clouds accumulating in the sky, a peacock in the garden spread its kaleidoscopic tail like an embroidered canopy and started dancing frenziedly.

Bajra accosted Ajatasatru in a slow and softened voice: "King!"

While sitting on the cot near her, Ajatasatru softly dragged his palm on her pale forehead and told: "Tell me queen."

Bajra held one of Ajatasatru's hands in tight embrace and told: "Tell me king whether this will be a son or a daughter?"

Ajatasatru was startled by her question and didn't know how to respond.

Bajra continued with her same, cruel and peevish interrogation: "Tell me king whether this will be a son or a daughter?"

Ajatasatru abruptly got up from her bed and marched into his secret chamber without responding to her nagging interrogation. Bajra screamed with an unbearable labour pain.

In Ajatasatru's blurring vision floated the darkness of the Rajagruha prison house like an insolvable enigma, an incurable curse.

So cruel was that 'future-tell!' Bajra's first born son shall usurp the throne by murdering his father. The expressions became harder and complicated on Ajatasatru's obdurate, stony face. Would he imprison the pregnant queen and throw her into the dark chambers of the prison house like he did to his father? Would he throw the newborn baby into the unfathomable depths of the dark well? Was it so impossible for him to destroy the baby in his own hands? If he could be so ruthless towards his father, then why could he not be equally cruel and savage with his child? Ajatasatru was getting torn by these conflicting thoughts and did not find a way out. They were weighing heavily on him, crushing his being with their indelible weight; he felt like getting pushed into a state of irresistible frenzy and madness, getting cleaved into multiple, irretrievable fragments of his composite self, getting torn into many shattered, unrecognizable scrambles of his own valiant image.

Bajra's screams were largely audible. The pains of pregnancy! The embryo wanted to manifest, tearing apart her uterus, to come into being, to grow bigger and bigger into the monstrous and ruthless image of a king. He would imprison Ajatasatru, throw him into the same dark chamber into which he had thrown Bimbisara. A cold, chilling shiver ran through Ajatasatru's spine. His limbs started trembling like palm fronds in frigid wintry rain. He was lost in strange hallucinations.

Suddenly, he heard someone's footstep in his closed chamber and hearing this sound, he came back to his senses and looked back. The prison guard Chanda stood before him with a downcast head, waiting for orders.

Ajatasatru asked: "What is the news, Chanda?"

Chanda answered: "Your Excellency! For the last three days the prisoner has not even been offered water. Today is the fourth day."

Ajatasatru's facial expressions became cruder. He asked Chanda in a rough voice: "Then what?"

Chanda said: "Your Excellency! I could hear the scream—Hey Son! Hey Rajagruha!"

******

From the queen's chamber came the deafening sounds of blowing conches and joyous celebrations. Bajra's screams had been hushed up long ago. The maid Basumati came in with hastened steps and told in an elated voice: "Great news King. The queen has given birth to a son. You may summon the minister and order him to arrange for royal celebrations in Rajagruha."

Chanda pleaded: "Give the orders king. Give the orders."

Ajatasatru looked once at the maid Basumati, and once at the prison-guard Chanda. Then like a moonstruck lunatic, he started running outside in a frantic desperation for something unknown. Streets after streets, chambers after chambers, steps after steps—Ajatasatru was running like an unstoppable maniac. Within no time, he reached at the entrance of the prison house. The guards saluted him, of course with notes of surprise in their eyes about the king's sudden, unexpected arrival.

He ordered with an impetuous voice: "Open the door, guard."

The two huge iron doors opened unwillingly with a bizarre, crackling sound. The atmosphere inside the chamber was terribly gruesome, dark and sinister. Crossing the greyish steps, Ajatasatru hysterically ran towards the murky chambers of the prison house.

Today, the father had understood the meaning of fatherhood.

The creator had always been benevolent and merciful. Like a baby, Ajatasatru would go and fall at his father's feet, would apologize to him with a tear-flooded face, would beg for mercy with a genuflected posture.

But he was a little too late. Bimbisara's lifeless body lied there on the floor like a piece of chopped wood from a tree. He had chewed one arm in irresistible hunger, like a wild animal injured with the hunter's arrows. A few drops of blood had flown from the injury and had coagulated into tiny, circular, reddish spots on the ground.

From the palace were audible the relentless blowing of conches and the maddening howl of the celebratory crowd. They signalled the birth of the prince.

******

Yadubansa[32]

It was Kumarapurnima[33]the next day. The whole of Dwaraka was revelling in full spirit; an unbounded vigour and enthusiasm had percolated through the whole atmosphere like an immense spread of sunlight on the darkened Earth. As a prelude to the main celebration, the Yadavas had started merrymaking on its streets. Under the intoxicating spells of wine, they had crossed all limits of decency and self-control and had become like a herd of mad dogs engaged in a scuffle over an abandoned piece of dry, desiccated bone. The festivity's madness had spread all through the city's nooks and corners, like an epidemic, an incurable blight.

Near the window of his palace, Srikrishna breathed out a long sigh of helplessness that diffused into the gloomy air within no time. He had not perhaps taught these Yadavas the assuaging mantra of self-control. For a moment, he felt as if History was mocking him on his face, ridiculing him with utter disdain and condescension.

Oh God! Akrura was saved by a fluke. Otherwise,

---

32   The Yady dynasty to which Srikrishna belonged.
33   A Hindu religious festival.

he would have been smashed to dust under the wheels of Satyaki's recklessly speeding chariot. An innocent baby was just now crumpled to an unrecognizable lump of flesh under Pradyumna's frantically racing chariot-wheels and nobody paid heed to that. Everybody was savagely engrossed in the maddening carnival that swept across the whole Yadava landscape like a ravaging flood. Satyaki and Pradyumna were engaged in a needless and absurd-looking charioting competition. The former laughed boisterously while passing ahead of the latter's chariot while the other Yadavas were thoroughly enjoying the ghastly scenario without any sense of shame or compunction. They started shouting loudly when Pradyumana now managed to go past Satyaki's chariot. The sharp and heartrending cry of the dead baby's mother was lost in that heinous, congregated laughter.

Srikrishna kept watching helplessly the self-destructive madness of the Yadavas.

Akrura breathed out a long sigh and paused for a moment. But he did not know how to console the mother who had lost her baby.

The mother was crying inconsolably: "Hey Krishna! Hey Yadava leader! Hey Dwaraka king! How can you so callously watch such madness of the Yadavas with open eyes?"

But who would answer her? The Lord himself was dumb and helpless today. His own plight was deplorably pitiful.

But the Lord was mysterious and enigmatic as usual. His mystery was inconceivable and indecipherable as well as inexplicable. But how could he silently witness such horrifying spectacle of the Yadavas' degradation? How could he not stop their moving steps towards self-destruction?

Akrura pondered deeply over this question and could not manage to find an answer. There was no end to his inquisitiveness; but it was all in vain.

He thought of asking the Lord today: "What is this new mystery, Lord?"

But he could not muster the courage to ask the Lord as his plight was pathetically deplorable. He was engrossed in deep and troubling thoughts and his usually bright forehead was today filled with immensely proliferating frowns. His dazzling body that had remained a perennial attraction for the gopis looked terribly lacklustre whereas his lotus-eyes looked pale and lifeless. His face was enshrouded with a feeling of appalling sadness and utter displeasure.

What a piteous and disconsolate condition of the Lord of the universe it was! The living epitome of mirth and vitality was today gravely saddened and dejected by a pestering thought that kept on haunting his otherwise serene and jovial psyche. Akrura had never witnessed the Lord in such an abject condition. The Lord who had always remained cool and unperturbed even in the midst of the enemies in the *Mahabharata*, the Lord who had imparted Arjuna the ultimate wisdom of life in the midst of a bloodied battlefield, the Lord who had maintained his serene composure in the midst of adversity, was so ungainly perturbed today. These thoughts greatly troubled Akrura's mind.

Akrura mustered some courage to ask him this

question and never left him until all his questions were answered. He thought he would fall at the Lord's feet, prostrate before him and not leave him until the latter did not clarify his doubts.

But Akrura still apprehended to enter into Srikrishna's dark, gloomy and secluded chamber caught in the whim of an inexplicable and craven terror. But when he managed to slowly enter into the room, he was flabbergasted at the Lord's uncanny, terrifying appearance. It was no more his delightful, soothing face that Akrura had mostly witnessed, but it was his violent, destructive image that floated before his eyes like the gruesome image of an unidentified catastrophe in the offing. This image was once seen by Uttanka; it was seen by Duryodhana and Arjuna in the battlefield of *Mahabharata*—the image that was bigger than the world, the universe, the image that stretched out into the void beyond the galaxies, the image that could engulf the whole of humankind in a gulp. Akrura pleaded: "O Lord! Relinquish this destructive image of yours. I do not have the courage to see it even once. I want to see you in your calm and reassuring image. I want to see you as a fellow Yadava, as a fellow Yadava shepherd. I never want to see you in this terrifying, cataclysmic figure."

For a moment, Akrura was lost in a trance and then he suddenly came to his senses. He did not really comprehend whether it was truth or an illusion? In a moment, the Lord reappeared before him in his reassuring human appearance. A wry, gentle smile splashed on his lips like a dazzling moon appearing for a moment in the cloud-infested sky. Akrura was reassured; he breathed out a long, comforting shy of relief and then he asked the Lord in an inquisitive voice: "I am reassured my Lord. But what is this deplorable plight of yours? I am not able to bear it even for a moment my Lord." Then Akrura prostrated before Srikrishna and asked in an almost asphyxiated voice: "Lord! Why are you playing this mystery with this miniscule, ignoble slave of yours? Why is this inexplicable gloominess camouflaging the usual and comforting delightfulness of your face? Your plight pains me a lot my Lord. It pains me a lot. I cannot bear it."

Srikrishna's calm and soothing face suddenly became uncharacteristically rough and cruel. The softness of his countenance suddenly disappeared. He said in an abrupt, cruel voice: "Leave Dwaraka this moment Akrura. Leave now. It's my order."

Akrura could not comprehend the meaning behind such sudden, cruel and inexplicable gesture on the Lord's part.

A cold shiver ran through his spine. Deeply saddened, he cried like an inconsolable baby and said and an almost asphyxiated voice: "What sin did I commit my Lord? I am no more than a dust particle under your feet. How can I leave Dwaraka without you?"

There was a faint glimmer of a smile in Srikrishna's lips.

Looking at poor Akrura's grievous plight, the Lord's voice turned soft, kind and commiserative for a moment. He answered in a mellowed voice: "I had told Arjuna in Kurukhsetra's bloodied battlefront that there is neither sin nor piety in my creation. All virtues and vices that human beings are endowed with are indeed inevitable parts of Nature. Nothing is absolute in this world; everything is relative. There is no body in this world who can be fully virtuous or fully vicious. The man who possesses both virtues ad vices is dear to me. That is my concept of an ideal man. You be that ideal man, Akrura. Then you can also become dear to me."

Akrura was thoroughly perplexed by such inane ambiguity in Srikrishna's tone and asked in a thoroughly stupefied voice: "Why do you give this ambiguous piece of advice to me, my Lord? I am not able to comprehend the undercover mystery lying hidden behind your sweet but convoluted explanation. What new mystery is this, my Lord?"

By now, the Lord's voice had completely softened and pacified. But it had now suddenly turned stoic and uncharacteristically dispassionate; there was neither harshness nor indifference in that detached voice.

Akrura was still perplexed by this newfound stoicism on the Lord's face. His expression and voice were turning more stupefied and anxiety-ridden. Akrura again fell on the Lord's feet and said: "Please stop this inconceivable mystery with me my Lord. I am not able to bear it."

With a gentle and disarming smile on his face, the Lord answered: "Why do you forget Akrura that I told Arjuna that my mystery is indecipherable?"

Akrura now wittily replied looking straight into the Lord's eyes: "My Lord! But I know you had also told Arjuna that the person who completely dedicates himself to you, you rescue him from the ineluctable quagmire of your mystery. I am completely devoted to you my Lord. I am your slave, your disciple, your devotee. Please rescue me."

The Lord's facial expressions turned cruel, uncompromising and brutally real. He said: "That is why I am telling you Akrura. Leave Dwaraka right now. I am telling you this for your good. This Dwaraka will be thoroughly decimated Akrura. I do not want you to be destroyed like an insect in that blazing inferno that this city is shortly going to turn into."

Akrura answered: "But my Lord! You are the creator and the destroyer. Can you not rescue your favourite Dwaraka and the Yadavas under the encompassing shade of your Sudarshana wheel[34]?"

Srikrishna answered in a cool and composed voice: "Do not forget my words Akrura. We are all the slaves of *time. Time* is omnipotent; it will sweep us with its current, with its unstoppable, violent stream rushing towards eternity."

Akrura then answered: "If that is the case my Lord, then how 'can a 'nobody' like me survive *time's* murderous onslaught, its excruciating cataclysm?"

Srikrishna assured Akrura with a soothing voice: "No Akrura! You are innocent; you are pious; you are devotional. You will be amongst the blessed few who shall survive this cataclysm and inhabit this beautiful Earth."

Akrura said: "But this beautiful Earth is meant for the Yadava heroes also, my Lord."

Srikrishna calmly answered: "Drunkenness with wine and arrogance is not a sign of heroism, Akrura; it's a sign of inglorious cowardice, a telltale sign of their progressive movement towards an inevitable fall. After

---

34   The Wheel that Lord Srikrishna held in his hand. By his order, the wheel severed the heads of the demons and the sinners.

our victory in *The Mahabharata*, the Yadavas have become more powerful, illustrious and irresistibly vainglorious as a race and of course, I have no qualms in admitting that their proliferating vainglory and unruliness was in a way entertained, nursed and deified by me . I am sure you know it more than anyone else that all this has happened because of me. But the power and glory that I had benevolently showered on them have now turned into blind and deleterious arrogance. They have lost their sanity and reason under its intoxicating spell. They have lost all their virtues and have become slaves of their dirty, ignominious senses. They have no more remained heroes and proud protectors of 'dharma': they have turned into slaves— slaves of their dirty, sublunary desire. I call him a hero Akrura who has mastered his senses enslaved his desire. I had taught this sermon to the Yadavas; but today they have been maddened by the unbounded augmentation of their power and glory. Why would they remember me now?"

But in any case, how could Akrura leave Dwaraka alone, without the Lord?

Akrura was preparing to resist when the Lord ordered him again in a stern and authoritarian voice: "You go from here Akrura. Let me contemplate. Do not disturb my tranquillity anymore. Please allow me to stay immersed in my aloofness and quietude. Yes, before you leave, please instruct my orderlies to open my gold stashes for the Yadavas."

Akrura said in a surprised voice: "But these drunken Yadavas will plunder your gold stashes my Lord. They will plunder them."

The same mysterious smile kept on floating on the Lord's lips like an indecipherable enigma. He answered in a curious voice: "Fire needs fuel to burn Akrura. Fire needs fuel to burn. How would their fire of arrogance burn without the fuel of wealth? How would they turn thoroughly blinded by arrogance?"

Akrura still could not comprehend the mystery behind Srikrishna's words. Dumbfounded, he started walking away as Srikrishna said from behind: "Spread this message along the streets of Dwaraka that Kokua[35] has arrived in the city as the ultimate destroyer of mankind. He will eat up everybody and thoroughly decimate the city."

"Kokua!" Akrura had never heard of such a name. Was it a ghost or a monster or something else? He pondered.

Srikrishna smiled and said: "But the Yadavas would know it well. It's a beast with dishevelled hair, dark skin, a sinewy, dirty body, a dangling out tongue, a pair of sunken eyes and a few sharpened, deleterious nails. It's Kokua. It's a living incarnation of death."

Akrura asked: "But O omniscient! O omnipotent! Can you not destroy that beast by your eternal powers?"

Srikrishna answered in a grave voice: "Akrura! I have told you already that even I am the slave of *time*. I am also a slave of destiny. I cannot change its course."

Srikrishna's orders were inviolable and there was no way Akrura could have defied them. He departed with a heavy, burdened and disconsolate heart. But while leaving, he was pondering over the insolvable mysteries woven by the ever-enigmatic Srikrishna.

The huge uproar of the revelling Yadavas was audible from the streets; it was an unpleasant furore, an

---

35   -An imaginary beast that was supposed to kill the Yadavas.

ignominious ruckus. It was a terrible irony that the Lord Srikrishna who once taught his favourite Yadavas the virtues of self-control was now abandoned alone in his chamber in the midst of an atmosphere of brooding despair and utter helplessness. In a dejected mood, the Lord got up and stood near the window holding one of its railings in his hand.

There was Ambarisha moving on a chariot with an abducted Yadava lady. Addicted to wine and women, Ambarisha had lost all decencies and restraints. The abducted girl was shouting in helplessness crying for help while this shameless abductor was laughing loudly holding her hand firmly in his own and gesturing to the crowd with a vainglorious heart about his incomparably beautiful, prized passion. The lady's hair was dishevelled; her dresses were torn; her breasts were uncovered and while trying to cover her breasts with one hand, she was shouting: "O Srikrishna! O Lord! You had once rescued Draupadi from humiliation in the Kaurava Court by providing her countless dresses. How can you see me denuded on the streets of Dwaraka? Save my dignity O Srikrishna. Save my dignity."

A wry and indifferent smile splashed on Srikrishna's lips for a moment and then vanished like lighting disappearing in the midst of clouds. Whose dignity he was supposed to rescue? Of this distressed lady? The Yadava ladies were also drunken to the throat; they had wilfully surrendered their dignity to this bunch of devious, inebriated men. With open bodies, they were inviting these drunken louts to disrobe them, to enjoy their half-revealed bodies to the full, to curiously explore into the forbidden recesses of their nudity. They did not have the piety of a Draupadi, neither did they have her wholehearted devotion and her impeccable sense of surrender to the Lord. Rather, they had wilfully offered themselves for the gratification of these Yadava men's lascivious desire. Whose dignity then Srikrishna would have rescued?

The Sudarshana wheel on his left hand was despairing to sever the head of the lecherous, drunken lout Ambarisha; but the Lord restrained it from doing so as the crying lady was also an implicit contributor to the defilement of the self-destructive Yadavas. There was no point thus in severing Ambarisha's head. Srikrishna thought that let the Yadavas destroy each other and the Sudarshana wheel shall sever only the last surviving Yadava's head. But that was to happen at a much later stage.

Srikrishna kept on quietly watching through the window the self-destructive Yadava carnival. Before his eyes, two drunken wrestlers killed each other in a lethal wrestling bout on the field. Breathing out a heavy sigh, he came back from the window and ascended onto his throne.

Placing his heavy forehead on his delicate palm, the Lord asked himself: "What shall be the final consequence of this Yadava race?" By his mysterious designs, he could finish off all the Kaurava enemies on *The Mahabharata's* battlefront. All the great Kaurava heroes including Bhishma, Drona, Karna, Duryodhana, Jayadratha . . . all of them are now no more than dust particles on Earth. After a few days, these Pandavas will also move to heaven. Only the Yadavas will remain. But will they survive the ruinous spell of this mad craving for power?"

Srikrishna had assured Arjuna that he will take multiple births, if required, to rescue the distressed from the exploiters. But now the Yadavas were no more a distressed race; rather, they had become the exploiters themselves and prompt violators of 'dharma,' and initiators of sacrilegious ways of life on Earth. That day his son Shamba humiliated the innocent monks on the streets of Dwaraka. Will the Yadavas respect the monks anymore? Will they uphold the glorious heritage of *The Mahabharata*? Srikrishna was deeply engrossed in these pertinent and disconcerting questions.

What crude joke destiny was playing with the Yadavas!

These Yadavas were once exploited and tortured by the mighty Kansa. Srikrishna did not hesitate to kill his own uncle to rescue them from his atrocities; he had also killed Kansa's favourite wrestlers Chanura and Mustika to protect them from their threat. He had imparted the knowledge of self-restraint and spirituality to these Yadavas for which they became an illustrious race on Earth endowed with the qualities of heroism, divinity and glory. Known as 'Bashneyas' and 'Andhakas,' they surpassed the 'kshatriyas'[36] in terms of their proliferating valour and glory. Even the pride of Duryodhana was nothing before their vainglory. But how could now Srikrishna have rescued them as they had flagrantly deviated from the path of virtue and spirituality, from the path of 'dharma'?

This was the same Srikrishna who had exterminated the mighty Kauravas from the face of Earth to establish 'dharma.' He also did not hesitate to eliminate his own Kaurava disciple Durdasa (the last surviving Kaurava, Gandhari's son) through deception. But for a moment, Srikrishna remembered Gandhari's curse that not even a trace of the Yadava race will remain on Earth. Srikrishna started trembling like a palm frond remembering the curse as he knew that her words would never go in vain. There

---

36   -People belonging to a warrior race.

were tears in his eyes as what he saw in his front was nothing but complete annihilation, an approaching apocalypse.

Today was perhaps the Yadubansa's dooms day. Srikrishna could not have resisted it. In a feeling of frantic desperation, he kept striking his forehead vigorously with his hand.

Like a flock of swans came into the room his eight wives: Rukmani, Satyabhama, Jambabati, Nagnajita, Mitrabanda, Sulakhsana and Sushila. Srikrishna's chamber was filled with their unmatchable beauty and fragrance. He smiled at them instantly; but there was no sense of perceivable delight in that smile; rather it was a dry, indifferent and wearisome expression of welcome that flashed on his face for a moment and vanished.

Rukmani stroked the Lord's hair with her gentle, delicate palm and asked: "What are these dangerous premonitions my Lord?"

Srikrishna answered: "You eight wives of mine are experts in reading premonitions."

But Satyabhama asked with a sullen face: "Why did you drive away your favourite disciple Akrura so ruthlessly from Dwaraka, my Lord? Was it appropriate?"

Srikrishna answered: "There cannot be an answer to every question, my dear lady."

Then Nagnajita asked: "Why Daruka is opening all of Dwaraka's gold stashes at your orders? The Yadavas are plundering them."

Srikrishna answered: "Don't you know there is 'Kumara Purnima' celebration in Dwaraka? How would the Yadavas gift each other then?"

At this, Rukmani blasted at Srikrishna and said: "Will they gift each other by plundering our jewelleries? Is this your justice my Lord?"

Srikrishna answered: "What is the difference between pearl and lac? I had taught the Yadavas to consider both as the same thing. And they are doing the same right now."

At this Jambabati said: "Nobody can beat you in words my Lord. But is not an undeniable fact that the Yadavas today have turned into a bunch of selfish plunderers and nothing else?"

Srikrishna answered: "To plunder others' wealth is the religion of the plunderers. If the Yadavas are plundering your wealth today, then they are remaining true to their religion. Why do you bother my dear?"

The eight wives knew that Srikrishna has always been an archetypal, mysterious talker like this. Nobody could beat him in argument. He will discover his own cryptic logic to disprove the opponent. Even the greatest logical person like Arjuna has not been able to beat him in arguments and has been entangled in the inextricable net of his mystifying arguments. How could these eight queens beat him in words?

Rukmani said: "We all know my Lord that you are unbeatable in argument. But would you please explain to us in simple terms the rationale behind your strange behaviour now?"

Srikrishna answered: "I have told you Rukmani there is not always an answer to every question. You please leave me alone and allow me to stay immersed in my own thoughts. What I need now is aloofness and tranquillity."

Emitting heavy sighs, the queens left his chamber. But Srikrishna's strange behaviour had tormented them, had deeply saddened them all. Srikrishna gave a parting smile at his women. But he knew quite well that now even they could be subject to abduction and ravishment by the Yadavas. The same Arjuna would be there with his Gandiba[37]; but won't be able to use it as Srikrishna would have abducted its magical powers by then.

Srikrishna was again engrossed in his plaintive thoughts.

The eternally tolerant Earth was also crying for help due to the atrocities inflicted on its serene body by these maddened Yadavas. But how could Srikrishna have destroyed his own gorgeous creation in his own hands? Arjuna's ethical dilemma in Kurukshetra's battlefront had also engulfed him. How could he have destroyed his own people? If that day he advised Arjuna to fight his kith and kin for the sake of 'dharma,' why could he not train himself accordingly and do the same today? "No! I cannot destroy my favourite Yadavas in my own hand." Srikrishna said to himself.

He left his throne and started loitering inside the room and explained to himself: "I had told Arjuna on the battlefront that if the mind and the intelligence of the human being are destroyed, then he will automatically be doomed. I have corrupted the Yadavas' minds; I shall finish their intelligence without which, they will turn self-destructive and I shall only be the indifferent watcher of their self-inflicted annihilation."

A slow and inaudible laughter from the Lord's

---

37   The name of Arjuna's bow.

mouth filled the chamber for a moment and then mingled in its gloom.

Srikrishna could hear the unruly footsteps of the Yadavas approaching on the stair. With an artificial expression of contentment, he sat on his throne and quietly waited for the Yadavas to come in. His conjecture was absolutely right; they were pouring inside the room in herds in the fear of Kokua.

With a gentle smile on his lips, Srikrishna asked: "What is the news Daruka? Why are you here leaving the 'Kumara Purnima' celebrations? Why are you here Manmatha? You Madhumatta? Where is the excitement of the Kumara Purnima celebration on your faces? Why are you so worried, Subahu?"

Subahu uttered only one word in a trembling voice: "Kokua! Kokua!" He could not utter anything more.

"Kokua!" Smiled Srikrishna and said: "I have never heard of any such beast."

"But Akrura told us while leaving Dwaraka that Kokua is coming to kill us all, to annihilate the whole of Dwaraka. Kokua is a beast with dishevelled hair, dark skin, a sinewy and dirty body, a dangling tongue, a pair of sunken eyes and a few sharpened nails!" Said Manmatha in a trembling voice.

But Srikrishna asked: "Have any of you ever seen that beast?"

Daruka answered: "The Kokua is roaming from house to house deep in the night. He was going to tear apart my chest the way you tore apart Hiranyakashyapa's[38]. The

---

38   A monstrous king in Hindu mythology whom Lord Bishnu killed by tearing apart his chest.

moment I got up to get my mace, it dissolved in the night without leaving a trace. I could not clearly see his face."

Everybody described their horrific experience of having confronted the Kokua in the night's darkness. But strangely, nobody had seen that beast yet. But how could have they seen it? It was coming stealthily in the darkest hour of the night, like a burglar and after slaughtering a few Yadavas and creating havoc in the city, it used to disappear like a ghost in the blinding depths of the night. That is why every house of Dwaraka was closed immediately after the evening."

Srikrishna feigned being terribly worried and said: "After the battle of *The Mahabharata*, you khsatriyas claim yourselves to be the best warriors on Earth. And then, you fear this unknown beast so much. Isn't it funny?"

Daruka answered in a fallen voice: "But this is Kokua!"

Madhumatta said: "My Lord! You are the saviour of the Yadava dynasty. Only your Sudarshana wheel can destroy the Kokua. How can we be destroyed when you are here in Dwaraka?"

Srikrishna answered: "I had also answered to Arjuna on this on Kurukhsetra's battlefront. Man is his own enemy, is his own friend and his own saviour. Have you all forgotten my words?"

"But as long as your Sudarshana is in your hand, whom should we fear my Lord?" Said one amongst the Yadavas.

Srikrishna answered in a gloomy voice: "After the *Mahabharata* battle, my Sudarshana is powerless. In the pogrom for 'dharma,' its power has diminished. Its only power remains for the last kill."

Feigning helplessness, Srikrishna explained: "The little power that Sudarshana has is to kill the last Yadava."

"Sudarshana is now powerless." Cried the Yadavas together in a sense of utter helplessness.

In a contrived tone of reassurance, Srikrishna told with a smiling face: "After the battle of *The Mahabharata*, you are the best worriers left in the world. You have earned great reputation on Earth in the name of 'Basneyas' and 'Andhakas.' Only you can destroy the Kokua. Now go and let me contemplate."

The Yadavas departed being contented with the assuring words of Srikrishna when he said: "Today is the full moon night. You be prepared for the dark moon night when you might have an opportunity to confront Kokua for the last time. But you need not fear at all for you are the Yadavas, the heroes."

The Yadavas responded in one voice: "Yes! Yes! Today we are the best khsatriyas in the world. Whom should we fear?"

Then the Yadavas departed. A small ray of smile flashed on Srikrishna's lips and then disappeared like a waning moon in the sky."

The shout of the revelling Yadavas on the streets of Dwaraka had now greatly intensified. They were holding maces and bows in their hands and making valiant protestations of their unmatchable valour and heroism. It was Kumara Purnima; the dark moon night was yet to come after fifteen days. Srikrishna has also assured them that they could kill Kokua.

On the sombre and crepuscular space of the city of Dwaraka, slowly descended the edacious shadows of the dark- moon night. Srikrishna kept staring at the calm, lifeless candle inside his chamber and got engrossed in deep, onerous thoughts. Outside, the Yadavas kept shouting: "Kokua," "Kokua." Their shout was so loud that it submerged the incessant barking of wild dogs and the jackals through the marauding silence of the night.

Somebody shouted: "Hey! There went the Kokua."

Another Yadava said: "Where? Where?"

The first one said: "I had caught him by his hair. But it slipped off my hand and he escaped."

Another Yadava shouted: "Mace! Mace! Where is my mace? The mace in which I had smashed the Kauravas to dust!"

Another one shouted: "Where is my bow? Where is my quiver? Where are my arrows? Oh! I have left them at home."

Srikrishna started laughing vociferously. He was assured now that the intelligence of the Yadavas was now completely destroyed. Now they were the slaves of their senses."

Somebody shouted in the dark: "Hey! Here escapes the Kokua! Catch it Subahu! Catch it."

From the crowd, Satyaki asked: "Where did it escape?"

Another voice answered in the dark: "Into the forest."

Satyaki shouted: "I will see who will rescue you the beast? I am the great warrior Satyaki."

The Yadavas started running into the dark forest to catch the Kokua."

"Here is the Kokua! Hit it." Somebody shouted and Shamba started hitting a Kadamba[39] tree in the dark thinking it to be the Kokua. In that hit, 'Kadambari[40]' started flowing from the tree like a stream.

Somebody from amongst the Yadavas shouted: "This is Kadambari. I had never tasted such sweet drink in my life. But where is the Kokua?"

"Oh! It's very sweet." Said somebody else from amongst the crowd.

Another one said: "Drink this Kadambari juice to the lees. Leave the Kokua and drink the sweet Kadamabri juice."

The Yadavas now had left the kokua and were madly drunk with the Kadambari juice. They did not have control over their senses anymore. In the obfuscating darkness of the night and bereft of their senses, they saw each other as Kokuas. Srikrishna stood beneath one Kadamba tree and enjoyed the rarefied scene of the Yadavas destroying each other in a strange, ghastly, suicidal act. Could his Sudarshana wheel ever have destroyed the Yadavas so easily?

Satyaki was shouting in darkness: "The Kokua escaped right in front of Shamba's eyes. If I was there in his place, I would have smashed it to death with my mace." There was a clandestine note of ridicule in his voice at Shamaba's inability to kill the Kokua.

---

39   -A tree in the subcontinent whose botanical name is **Neola-marckia Cadamba**.

40   -The juice of the Kadamba tree.

Shamba retorted in a taunting voice: "I know about your heroism in the battle of *Mahabharata*, Satyaki."

Satyaki answered by twisting his moustache: "How can you forget my heroism in that battle, Shamba? I had alone penetrated through Dronacharya's *chakrabyuha*[41] circle when nobody else could dare to do it. I am the real war-hero of *The Mahabharata*. It is only because of Srikrishna's propaganda that Arjuna is being hailed as *Mahabharata's* greatest worrier."

Shamba answered: "Hey Satyaki! How can you forget that Bhurishraba held you by your hair and it's only me who rescued you from his clutch. How can you forget that?"

Satyaki answered to Shamba's taunt through a vigorous blow of his sword. Satyaki's severed head rolled on the soil at a distance.

Leaving Kokua, Pradyumna came running towards Satyaki to attack him. Satyaki collapsed on the ground being hit by Pradyumna's arrows.

Then started a full-fledged war amongst the Yadavas themselves. There were attacks and counter-attacks with mace, with swords and spears, with arrows . . . The whole battlefront was filled with cries and shouts and screams.

At the end of that sickening and abysmal dark night, the faint, pubescent light of the dawn was blooming in the sky and spreading all over its languid body like rejuvenating, whitish colouration. The colossal body of the dark forest that was laid stretched out like an abandoned corpse was slowly getting illuminated by the flooding

---

41   -A circular pattern woven by the soldiers in the battlefield whom the enemy soldiers could not penetrate so easily.

deluge of the sunlight. Inside the forest and on the ground, lied scattered the bodies of the slain Yadavas which created the illusion of another Kurukshetra battlefield.

Srikrishna looked at the appalling scene with a desolate heart and saw his favourite son Pradyumna sitting beneath a 'kadamba' tree and wailing inconsolably looking at the bodies of his fellow Yadavas.

Pradyumna was a great and powerful worrier. But why should he have survived from Yadubansa's destruction? Srikrishna ordered his Sudarshana: "Sudarshana! Go and finish your last job." In a moment, it severed Pradyumna's head and came back to Srikrishna's hand.

Srikrishna said: "No! I do not need you anymore, Sudarshana. All my tasks have been completed. Now I have to endure the consequences of my own deeds. You are no more needed for me."

Saying this, Srikrishna threw it off from his hand.

The golden top of the Dwaraka city was slowly getting ignited into a resplendent display of effervescence with the blooming sun's light. For the last time, Srikrishna looked at the bodies of his favourite sons—Shamba, Aniruddha, Pradyumna and others and smiled curiously staring at the blossoming sun in the sky.

Then with a calmly dejected disposition, he started heading in an uncertain direction.

In his front, was spreading the green forest— unperturbed and soothing like death itself.

******

A Moonlit Night in Spring

It was already past 12 o' clock in the night. Hrudaya Babu was still not able to sleep even after consuming two 'calmpose' tablets. No! They did not work anymore; they had become totally ineffective. A little while ago, the sound of a drunkard's moving feet was faintly audible from the empty road. . . Certainly, he was returning from an alcohol-club; his feet moved unsteadily, sometimes to the left, sometimes to the right making a low, clattering sound that dissolved in the darkness like a distant, unclear music. That sound in the tranquil night reverberated in Hrudaya Babu's mellowed ears and disturbed his sleep, periodically. He felt at least something worthwhile was happening in his otherwise dull, companionless and uneventful life. At least, there was a living human being in his vicinity and this feeling infused some kind of a reinvigorating and buoyant spirit into his otherwise sterile, desolate and woebegone heart. The sound slowly dissolved in the quiet night like a dissoluble pill in a glass of water.

Outside, was spread the spring night's crimson moonlight like a golden sheet enshrouding the darkened

Earth, that was lying out there, across the dark night's sprawling space, like an abandoned corpse. Through the right-side window, a lurid splash of that light fell scattered on Hrudaya Babu's wide, spread-out chest. A portion of it was also spilled on the empty bed, incongruously diffused into its floridly embroidered coverlet.

Time is very strange . . . One day this beautiful moonlight ignited fire in Hrudaya Babu's excited nerves and tendons combusting them in the flames of desire. Even today, it rejuvenates his mind and spirit despite his sick body, his approaching old age and his proliferating infirmity. The same moon light, the same spring night, the same hypnotizing south-wind! That day, this moonlight became a dazzling ornament on the soft, sensuous body of Hrudaya Babu's bride and filled his mind with irrepressible, youthful vigour and vitality. But now she has grown old and feeble, and has taken customary recourse to compulsive spirituality. She spends most of her time in 'Puja[42]' and other spiritual activities inside the worship-room and once on bed, she starts chanting God's name relentlessly till sleep descends into her eyes like the former's heavenly blessing and closes them down with its soothing, assuasive spell. At times when Hrudaya Babu gets a little naughty and sleazy with her for a change, what shrilling, cacophonic and repellent sound she makes! "S h a m e l e s s fellow! Characterless fellow! Get lost;" she shouts.

Thank God! These days, she is on a leisurely pilgrimage to Puri, to bathe in the sacred sea, and to see Lord Jagannath's holy face and to stay happily immersed in her phantasmagoric, spiritual world. She is there for the last two days, and expectedly, would spend a week there.

---

42   Worship of any Hindu god or goddess.

And for Hrudaya Babu, this week is supposed to be one of unbounded freedom, of enjoyable freakishness, of quizzical ventures. But what great adventure could he have ventured into with the meaningless freedom of this arthritis-ridden, frail body? He could only look at this ticklish moonlight of spring with gaping eyes and ruminate over his lost, days of grandeur and romanticism . . .

But still, this short-lived freedom, this profligate liberty is alluring and attractive. Now he does not have to worry about his wife's trenchant admonitions: "Take medicine on time." He no more has to fear the irksome ghosts of diabetes and hypertension. He does not have to read *Geeta* or *Bhagabata* compulsively sitting on his wheel chair; neither does he have the coercion to sit beside an obnoxious 'Baba' caught from somewhere by his wife and bow to the strange and bizarre rules laid down by him. There is no shout from his wife, neither is there any screeching, ear-splitting allegation of being a shameless, characterless fellow by her when he sits restfully with his whiskey bottle on the chair.

But on the contrary, this aloofness, this alienation is also a torment. There is some satisfying sense of companionship even in a skirmish with the wife; there is a gratifying feeling of completeness even in this acute and deteriorating conjugality. After Surama Devi has gone on pilgrimage, a terrible sense of loneliness has completely captivated Hrudaya Babu like a conjuring spell of hypnotism cast on him by a wicked magician.

This moonlit night of spring! This fickleness of this south-wind! This lifelessness! This aloofness! And this paralysed body! Hrudaya Babu felt a sharp sting of pain in the inmost recesses of his soul.

Vexed and agonized by the pangs of aloofness, he took out a cigarette-case from beneath his pillow and tried to light a cigarette. These days he finds it difficult to light one, alone by himself. The fickle gushes of wind barging in through the window like unwelcome trespassers extinguished the matchsticks once they were lighted. After trying hard for many times, Hrudaya Babu finally succeeded in lighting a cigarette, inhaled a mouthful of smoke, and then, exhaled some of it bearing a stoic, concocted expression on his face. The smoke coiled into the atmosphere in an exquisite, circular trajectory and looked like a white spectre, carved in the air, against the crimson canvass of the moonlit night. Hrudaya Babu felt like conquering a hitherto unconquered mountain range.

Who shall believe that during his younger days, Hrudaya Babu was a tireless hunter? Who can imagine that he roamed through the mountains with a rifle in his hands, day in and day out and spent most of his life in the jungles and hills as a forest-conservator?

In the immense tranquillity of the night, the sound of someone's footsteps kept approaching his vicinity through chequered gloom of the garden. No! It was perhaps an illusion, the semblance of a sound —he thought. A few street dogs roaming helter-skelter barked vigorously into the labyrinthine depths of the night. Listening to their bark, an Alsatian dog in the neighbourhood reciprocated and barked with equal vigour and savagery. It barked for some time and then, stopped while everything became quiet again.

Hrudaya Babu regressed into his past laden with roiled assemblages of wistful and morbid memories coupled with exultant and happy ones. With the abject sterility of this paralysed body, he could not imagine that one day he possessed a joyous and exuberant youth, that one day he could dream of impossible things and could achieve many of them.

Those days, his nights were spent in the empty, marooned bungalows surrounded by the dark, ubiquitous and pervasive forest. But even once, he didn't feel the pangs of aloofness in the brooding and vicious emptiness of his surroundings, quite astoundingly though. The forest's beauty had mesmerized him. The golden deer's luscious eyes had maddened him into an interminably seductive frenzy.

But Hrudaya Babu could not write a single poem in his life. He had tried many times; but he never liked his own poems. He could never captivate his heartfelt feelings correctly on pen and paper, by adorning them with multitudes of decorative similes and metaphors. Hrudaya Babu kept on tearing off and throwing away his poems, one after another, every now and then.

But still, he has always remained a dreamy, romantic, and poetic mind.

Caught in the maze of multitudes of divergent, embroiling thoughts, Hrudaya Babu suddenly spotted the blurry and darkish silhouette of a human head outside his window; and was shaken from inside at the sight of such hazy and bloodcurdling spectacle. He got up with a jerk. Though initially he did not comprehend much of the frightening proceedings in the garden's dark and muddled environment, he could sense immediately afterwards that the man was actually cleaving the grill-wires with a cutter. Its sound was faintly audible.

Hrudaya Babu understood instantly that this man was either a thief or a dacoit. It was no use calling his servant Mangulia as he usually slept deep, like a modern-day Kumbhakarna, and hardly responded to his call despite its unmatchable vociferousness. He required a fire-brigade bell to get up from sleep. Hrudaya Babu conjectured that he must have smoked opium and fallen deep asleep somewhere, having gotten comatosely inebriated by the intoxicating spell of this narcotic material. He attempted to pull out his revolver from below his bed, but quickly remembered that it was not loaded. Surama Devi was always appallingly discomfited by the awareness of a loaded revolver's sheer presence beneath the bed-cushion. Then what was the use of keeping a revolver? But she never understood the logic; neither did she try to understand.

By this time, the man had entered inside the house by cutting the window-grill.

Hrudaya Babu switched on the bed light and in the electric bulb's faint glimmer, could see a dark and moribund silhouette materialize into an ugly and gruesome human figure, right in front of him. He first got terribly scared, but then regained his composure due to his vast experience and his lately cultivated indifference and stoicism towards life. The man wore a short, worn-out black pant; his wide, open chest was filled with wavy, undulating hairs and a quadrangular locket hung inchoately from his neck by a crummy and greasy black thread. He had a huge and curly black moustache coiling below his nose like a dark, venomous snake and a dirty handkerchief circled around his head like a dark, smudgy cover enshrouding an abandoned corpse. Hrudaya Babu thought that the man is a new recruit to the profession of larceny.

The man was also startled to see Hrudaya Babu right in front. He might not have expected someone in the house to be awake so late in the night. Hrudaya Babu thought: "Let him loot and plunder whatever he likes. I don't have the strength to stop him. But let me at least enjoy a man's relishing companionship in the midst of this brooding and tortuous aloofness.

Hrudaya Babu told: "Hey man! Sit here. Why do you get so desperate? I am giving you the keys of this steel cupboard. You do not need to take out your knife or something and threaten me. You are actually the rich people's friend. But unfortunately they call you a dacoit. You take comfortably whatever you want. But before that, come and sit with me and help me light my cigarette. Let's sit down and talk. Do you fear I will call the police? See! The telephone lies there, dead, at a distance. Moreover, I am a disabled man. So, you need not worry. Please sit on that wheel chair. There is no other chair nearby."

That man was shocked and flabbergasted to hear such kind, friendly and compassionate words from a house-owner, at the backdrop of such an unusual and unexpected encounter. Then he sat quietly, as per the latter's endearing instructions, on the wheel chair without uttering a single word. Then he lighted his own cigarette and also Hrudaya Babu's.

On the road, a speeding car almost met with an accident. In the indistinct gloom of the night, it would have crushed into the roadside sewage; but the driver put the break right in time. But the rugged creak of its wheel rubbing against the scabrous and bumpy soil was largely audible through the night's immense and deathlike tranquillity.

The man suddenly got up from the chair, took out

a knife from his pocket, brandished at Hrudaya Babu and said in an aggressive tone: "Keys . . ."

Hrudaya Babu said in an unruffled voice: "Keep that knife in your pocket, friend. I told you don't need to brandish your knife or anything at me. The keys are with my wife who is now in Puri. See below the pillow. There might be a duplicate key."

Heedless of Hrudaya Babu's words, the man kept on brandishing the knife uninterruptedly at him, inserted his left hand below the pillow and extracted the duplicate key dangling from a dazzling, metallic key-ring making a faint, jingling cadence which clashing against another key in the same ring. Then he opened the steel cupboard and went on scrambling through the racks with both hands, desperately, like a moonstruck lunatic. There was no other thing in the brief case except a few crumpled, neglected, wasp-infested, dust-ridden papers.

Yet, there was no sense of fear or apprehension on Hrudaya Babu's face; rather he thoroughly enjoyed the scene and relished its preposterous farcicality. In the meanwhile, the burglar kept on examining two fixed-deposit forms in the dim light. Hrudaya Babu said; "Hey friend! You will get bundles of currency notes in the steel cupboards of ministers and leaders. They don't keep them in banks to evade income tax. But all our money is in the bank. Those two pieces of paper will be of no use for you. Those are fixed deposit forms."

The burglar threw the forms on the ground with a visible expression of disgust and indignation, and went on scrambling desperately for something more in the shelves and in the brief case. To his greatest delight, he discovered a gold necklace and two finger-rings inside the brief case; his incisive, razor-sharp eyes lit up with blistering excitement.

Hrudaya Babu told: "Friend! If you kindly spare that necklace, I will be greatly obliged. It is my younger daughter Sujata's. She is now with God. I had bought it for her the day she first went to college, elatedly, and stepped into its premise with lots of joy and excitement. She used to go there wearing this necklace, with a happy and contented disposition markedly visible on her face; she relished wearing this necklace."

Reminiscing his dead daughter, Hrudaya Babu drew a huge, voluminous breath into his lung and paused for a moment like a lifeless effigy, with its stone-carved eyes looking pensively still and immovable. Then, he stared into the nocturnal, moonlit air with an expression of consummate stoicism; within a moment, his stare decocted the night's self-indulgent, juvenile fickleness into a maturely grievous expression of intense grief. By that time, the man had splayed the whole floor with almost all of Surama Devi's costly sarees from the cupboard, and with some of Hrudaya Babu's elegant and gaudy ironed dresses. The gold necklace and the finger-rings had by that time slipped into his pant pocket.

In the bedroom's dim blue light, one vodka and two whiskey bottles dazzled flickeringly in the cupboard's polished and glistening shelf. The man had already taken out the vodka bottle, but Hrudaya Babu told: "Don't bring that one, my friend; I don't have tomato juice and there is no soda either. If they were there, I would have made excellent bloody-merry cocktail for you. Even today, I am known for making excellent cocktails, my friend. Rather you bring that whiskey bottle. It can be drunk with water. This is not your cheap, country-made liquor. This is sophisticated foreign scotch. It's the customs thing, you know."

That man held the Vat-69 bottle in his hand and sat on the sofa, heedless of Hrudaya Babu's continual interactions with him in the form of an amicable and friendly chatter.

Hrudaya Babu told: "The adjacent room is the dining hall. Please take a little trouble, my friend and bring two glasses along with one water-bottle."

The man obliged unhesitatingly.

He hurriedly poured three pegs of whiskey into the glass and started drinking them in the mad desperation of a terribly thirsty man. Perhaps, that is how he drank his alcohol-- to gulp large pegs at one go, without even water. Presumably, he was not accustomed to measured pegs and did not require water at all for drinking his alcohol. He finished off the glass in a single breath, and then lighted a cigarette. Hrudaya Babu, contrarily, poured a peg of whiskey, and then some water into his glass, and then, started sipping from it in smaller gulps.

Hrudaya Babu said: "The flavour of scotch is different my friend."

Next time, the man poured a lot more into his glass, leaving perhaps only one peg in the bottle.

But suddenly, they heard from the road frequent, screeching whistles from the patrolling police van rambling through the condensed dark of the night like a giant, nasty vermin. The man became aghast and serious and got worried out of fear and a note of momentary, panicky apprehension floated on his face, and then precipitated into an inchoate cluster of furrows and frowns. As per recent newspaper reports, some 'khalistani[43]' terrorists had encroached into the city, and the police were frantically searching for them in the suspect area. The combing operations had intensified of late, and was supposed to continue ad-nauseam till dawn.

The man switched off the light.

Hrudaya Babu still kept on relishing the man's proximity, even though he was purportedly a notorious burglar. For a long time, he had not enjoyed anybody's gratifying and heart-warming company, over a few pegs of whiskey, in an amicable, unselfish conversation. He hardly had occasion for such intimate one-to-one interaction except with specialist doctors over his persistent and chronic medical conditions.

With a whiskey-filled glass in his hands, Hrudaya Babu's auspicious night-friend had become completely oblivious of the former's presence in his vicinity. Perhaps he felt a little uneasy, awkward and discomfited in the house-owner's presence.

"The man doesn't know how to talk in a decent and relaxed manner" — thought Hrudaya Babu, eliciting a little not discontent on his expressive face, particularly because of the man's dull, sterile and stubborn unresponsiveness to his words. In single gulps, the man had finished off large pegs and then, had started casting his avaricious and predatory eyes rapaciously on the other bottle lying forlorn on the cupboard's gaudy and glittering shelf.

Hrudaya Babu told him: "Quickly change your black short pant, 'night-friend.' I know you won't reveal

---

43   The Sikh terrorists of Punjab who wanted a separate land form them known as khalistan.

your name to me; so, I call you 'night-friend' without any decent and proper name of yours available to me, right at the moment. Now if you venture outside with this tarnished short pant, this foreboding pair of dark glasses and with this gigantic, bull's figure, then you will encounter the real danger. People might think you are a dacoit. That's why please obey my instructions. Please change your dresses."

The 'night-friend' wilfully obliged. He kept the whiskey glass on the table and changed his dresses quickly.

Hrudaya Babu emitted another mouthful of smoke into the air and said: "That's better. You now look like a thorough gentleman imbued with refined and modern etiquettes. Ha! This figure! These so called gentle or savage figures! All are tailor-made. Your attire makes you either a gentleman or a savage. Now if someone spots you in this renewed apparel, would he ever imagine that you encroached into my house as a plunderer, in the blinding depths of the night, by cutting the gate's grills? Now you look either like a sophisticated leftist intellectual or an accomplished artist, 'night-friend.' Cheers . . . ."

Now, the 'night-friend' responded, and responded with a surprising note of impeccable vehemence and authority. Breaking the dark night's inglorious monotony, he spoke in a grave, whiskey-drunken, and inebriated voice: "Ha! For your kind information, I am a postgraduate from a university. M. A. in Political Science . . . Yet, I am unemployed, jobless."

Hrudaya Babu responded in a taunting note of sarcasm: "Then you must have cleared your examination through malpractice. Right?"

The 'night-friend' retorted angrily: "So what! That

is the universally acceptable practice everywhere today. You pass the examination either by malpractice or through some other connection. But my certificate is genuine."

The 'night-friend' continued: "I have appeared in many job interviews, but could not succeed in one. I remained unemployed for long. Then once I heard a minister pontificate in one of his inspirational harangues that our young men should invent their own ways and means for self-employment in a scenario where the government is not able to generate adequate employment opportunities for them. I got inspired and discovered this potent method of self-employment—burglary. Now this is my career, my illustrious career."

After telling this, the 'night-friend' inhaled a long, deep breath, and sat on the sofa flaunting a gesture of casual heedlessness on his face.

Hrudaya Babu remained speechless.

The 'night-friend' went on: "But you disappointed me a lot, my friend."

Hrudaya Babu enquired: "How? How did I disappoint you after offering so much of congenial and affable hospitality?"

The 'night-friend' answered: "After specializing in grill-cutting, I came here with the thrilling anticipation of plundering lots of wealth. I had gotten prior information that that you are suffering from paralysis and you spend most of your time being seated on a wheelchair. Your pious, devoted and world-renouncing wife is on a pilgrimage to Puri. Your servant is a perennial and compulsive opium-addict. The myth that floated in the air about you is that as a retired forest-conservator, you have amassed lots of wealth inside your gold-stash buried in some unexplored, secluded corner of your house. I had imagined that the plundered wealth from the forest's womb, from the infinite riches of Nature's bountifulness lies concealed somewhere, like a dark and unexplored secret, inside your stuffy and grandiloquent house. But whatever little I find here is just chickenfeed. You don't have a sandal-wood cot in your bedroom; neither do you have expensive jewelleries hidden in your gold-stash. Or is it your strategy, your witty shrewdness? Have you dug your wealth somewhere else to befuddle burglars like us? Does a dacoit burgle into someone's house in this blinding night's opaque darkness to engage in a gentle and cordial conversation with the owner over a few pegs of whiskey? To exchange pleasantries? Nonsense! My whole night is spoiled."

The night-friend tucked an addendum to his little harangue and said: "After my ceremonious entry into the profession of larceny, I had never confronted such terrible disillusionment in my life. Encroaching into your house, after the accomplishment of an arduous and painstaking grill-cutting exercise, looks to me an absolute disaster now.

Hrudaya Babu extended his heartfelt commiserations to his night-friend and answered: "You trust me, my friend. Whatever I may be, I am not at all shrewd, cunning or duplicitous in my demeanours. I kept on hunting through the forest all my life. When the hunter and the beast confront, no shrewdness works, my friend. Either you kill it or it will kill you. My whole life was spent running after the mysterious, feral animals of the jungle. I was enchanted by the enigma of the forest, my friend, by its splendiferous beauty, by its incandescent charm. I spent all my time, all my life pursuing the forest's unrevealed secrecies, its unending expanses of abstruse and mindboggling mysteries. How could I then have made for myself sandal-wood cots? Then also my friend, we are people of the older generation. We are not adept in this nasty and abominable craft of stealing. We filled the forests with sandal-wood plantations. Now these wood-mafias smuggle them, and sell them to the corrupt govt. officials who make expensive cots from the smuggled timber."

Outside, the sound of the patrolling police vans intensified in the form of an implicit, cautionary admonition to Hrudaya Babu's night-friend that he should be in the hiding. A motor cycle passed by making a loud and ear-splitting noise, emitting volumes of greasy, blackish smoke into the air.

Perhaps this was the policemen's last round of patrolling. Some early morning birds twittered indiscriminately on some distant tree's branches, and then became astonishingly silent, as if being captivated by the early morning's mysterious and bewitching calmness. The moon had waned sufficiently in the sky that was patiently waiting for the sun to bloom like an effulgent lotus on its all-pervasive, empyrean firmament. The vaulted sky was slowly getting filled with rambling and diffused blotches of faint, greyish patches prolonging like widening scars on its fecund body. In a few moments, those patches slowly turned red with the blooming sun's diffusive, nascent rays. In the meanwhile, the 'night-friend' had almost finished the second whiskey bottle.

On the main road, the thunderous sound of a moving truck was staggeringly audible.

Hrudaya Babu had finished the last peg. His eyes had gotten heavier with obtund and benumbing sleepiness.

In a drowsy and drunken voice, he told: "If you come another time 'night friend' when my wife is not here, I will prepare bloody-merry cocktail for you in my own hands." But he could hear no response. He managed to force away his drowsiness and look round. The 'night-friend' had escaped by jumping over the gate. He had left on the bed Sujata's necklace and finger-ring.

Hrudaya Babu lifted them, squeezed them tightly in his scraggy, tremulous hand and suddenly became uncharacteristically serious and sentimental. For some time, he went on caressing the gold necklace with his hand and emitted a long, deep breath from his lungs, while two unruly teardrops rolled down across his beardy, frown-ridden cheek like two tiny, sparkling gemstones falling from his eyes. Perhaps they were the two sublunary remnants of his dead daughter Sujata's erstwhile earthly presence. His warm, temperate sigh infused some sultriness into the cold and freezing breeze of the wintry dawn.

His two eyes were slowly getting closed . . .

*****

Bread and Moon

For the last one month, a strike of the labourers' union had been going on in the textile mills of the capitalists.

Despite all attempts of the rival union and the mill owners and in spite of enormous pressure from the govt. machinery, the strike kept on gathering unbelievable strength and momentum.

One could not but admire the local communist leadership's role in upholding the strike.

Comrade Vinod had drained himself off all his energy in relentlessly roaming through the labourer-slums, in encouraging the slum-dwellers to participate in the strike, in collecting funds, in arousing the slogan "long live the red flag" and in roaming around the city in different rallies. After returning from work, he exhaustedly slept on a few pamphlets and on a piece of newspaper inside a small room of the party office. He fell deep asleep.

After some time Comrade Lalita entered into the room. Comrade Lalita—a slim-figured, soft-spoken person and a good writer! Her responsibility was to evaluate on a regular basis all the English circulars and books of the party. She also worked as the editor of its weekly journal. Because of the strike, she was also entrusted with another responsibility — writing the bulletin.

This small and stuffy room was in fact Comrade Lalita's office. She came inside and switched on the light. A small table lied adjacent to the western window. There were dusty piles of papers and files lying scattered on its unclean surface which were further piled with newspapers on them. On the wall were hanging three equal sized photographs — in the middle was Marx, on the left was Stalin and on the right, was Lenin; there were dunes of dust accumulated on those old photographs.

There was also an old calling bell lying out there on the heap of paper on the table. Lalita pressed that bell three times with her finger.

The office boy Ramu came rushing in. Ramu was also a comrade, the only son of a labourer!

Lalita told in a softened voice: "Ramu! Coffee."

Ramu left listening to her order.

The dazzling moon had soared high up into the sprawling, bluish firmament of the sky. Towards the endpoint of the factory area, there was situated the party office. A zigzag red-pebbled road ran near the window in a sluggish, serpentine movement towards the dusty horizon. Sometimes one would find a bullock cart moving along that road with its slothful, gigantic wheels making bizarre, creaking sounds whereas at other times, one could trace one or two passersby walking along slovenly towards the distant villages. On the other side of the road, there laid an uneven rocky field elongating shapelessly towards the dusky and distant line of the horizon.

The tranquil but mesmeric moments of that indolent night were scented with the -sweet fragrance emanating from an unknown flower bloomed somewhere in the dark.

Lalita switched off the light inside the room with a mixed feeling of exhaustion and irritation.

One thin, crimson ray of the moonlight from outside had fallen imperceptibly on her; it had filled every remotest corner of her delighted soul with an unspeakable fullness and contentment. For a moment, she thought that the human history had witnessed many bloodied revolutions and many fierce conflicts; but there could never have been an end to this beautiful moon-blanched evening; there could never have been a pause to this evening's immense, unrestricted spread of joy.

Lalita switched on the light again. But in a moment the shabbiness of the room and prolonged training of her profession made her aware that enjoying Nature's beauty was nothing but escapism — counter-revolutionary bourgeoisie luxury.

Comrade Vinod had started snoring loudly.

Lalita had not seen Vinod yet. She was surprised by the sound of his snoring and listening to that sound, she looked in that direction. Vinod was wearing a pair of half-cleaned trousers and a half-shirt. On his feet were a pair of tattered 'kabuli' sandals; and on his half-torn shirt, there were stuck a party badge and the picture of a sickle and a hammer as the party's insignia.

Ramu brought a cup of coffee. Lalita ordered for another cup. Ramu left.

Lalita did respect Vinod a lot for his leadership

qualities and for his good knowledge and understanding of Marxism. Vinod could easily recite all the important quotations from Marx during a simple conversation. Once he had fallen in love with a girl and she had also reciprocated sufficiently and the marriage was almost to be completed as per the Vedic, Indian tradition. But the girl's father was a pure and unadulterated bourgeoisie, a staunch anti-Marxist. He made it adequately clear right at the beginning that he could tolerate his son-in-law becoming a disciple of Lord Sri Chaitanya[44], but could never endure his allegiance to the sickle & hammer . . .

Vinod had to return empty-handed. But intriguingly, his disappointment was not for his failed courtship, but for the fact that the communist party had lost a committed girl like Lila whose contribution for its growth and proliferation would have been immense. But even today Vinod did not forget to send party bulletins to Lila on a regular basis. Yet when any friend of his occasionally poked gentle fun at his failed courtship, Vinod promptly retorted by quoting Marx that "Nothing is being; everything is becoming." meaning "Nothing is still; everything moves." In the Marxist dialectic, a failed courtship was not something to be pitied and ridiculed as it was no more than an uneventful episode of life.

Ramu brought another cup of coffee. Lalita woke up and tipped Vinod's forehead in a soft, girlish touch.

Vinod woke up with a jerk, rubbed indiscriminately his sleepy eyelids and sat languidly on the newspaper heap.

Lalita asked: "Would you mind a cup of coffee, Comrade?"

---

44   A Hindu religious leader of the 16th Century.

Vinod's eyes and face lit up with the joy of some unexpected achievement.

He said: "Thank you Comrade."

Both of them sat near the table. Lalita lifted the coffee cup onto her lips and started sipping from the cup with a sense of delight and contentment on her face. Both went on sipping coffee form their respective cups.

Outside, the blooming moon had luxuriantly spread its crimson light all around. On the other side of the road, was an uneven hinterland elongating vaguely into the murky depths of the horizon.

The pebbly field lied ahead like an unclear thought. From there one could hear the intoxicating symphony of Raag Nageswari[45] from some body's flute playing somewhere in darkness.

Vinod asked; "Has tomorrow's bulletin gone to the press for printing, Comrade Lalita?"

Lalita did not pay heed to Vinod's inquiry and was contemplating a romantic poem in her mind:

"O moon! Between you and me the distances disappear!

O my love! Enamoured I am by your beauty and your attire!

Come to my window O divine beauty! Come to my window!

Kiss me my love and cuddle me in your embrace!"

Unaware of her romantic thoughts, Vinod said: "Comrade Lalita! Arrangements have been made for a

---

45   A classical musical note

huge gathering of party workers tomorrow evening. From the next day onwards the other mill workers of the locality are joining the mass strike. Your bulletin must be sharp and penetrative like a fired bullet. Could you please compose a chorus for tomorrow's meeting?"

Lalita became conscious and asked with a tone of curiosity: "What kind of a song, Vinod? Would you please clarify?'

Vinod sung in a dull and dispassionate voice:

"O Marx! The father of Communism!

On a barren soil did you sprout crops,

And gave food to the starving multitude."

Listening to Vinod's badly composed, unromantic poem, Lalita started laughing boisterously.

Vinod asked in an embarrassed voice: "Why did you laugh, Comrade Lalita"?

Lalita abruptly answered: "No reason! I just laughed like that."

Vinod hastily took out a cigarette from his pocket and lighted it.

Lalita stared looked at the portrait of Marx with a feeling of exhaustion and depression, and then said while addressing him: "Hey Marx! Your *Economical Interpretation of History* has converted human beings into machines, into pigs. Life for him is all about bread and butter, and nothing else. You have taught man only to eat and eat and eat. In his hungry pair of eyes, you have made this piece of bread look more beautiful than the translucent moon floating in the sky like a golden eagle with crimson wings. You have made money the ultimate goal of life. But there can be a greater goal than that of money. Have you ever spoken about that?"

Vinod threw that half-burnt cigarette out of the window and uttered in a grave voice: "I have been observing for quite some time comrade that you are progressively becoming an escapist. Freud calls this escapism a death instinct—the gist of Buddhism. The tendency to lose yourself in a huge vacuum is nothing but a mental weakness, a bourgeoisie luxury, a spiritual stagnancy. In the words of Erick Fromm, it's the 'terrorism of freedom'."

Laita got a little irritated from inside. She could no more tolerate these self-less, bookish machines. They thought as if the words of Marx, of Freud, of Fromm were everything in life. Whatever lied outside their propositions was all weak, absurd, bourgeoisie luxury.

Lalita answered: "I have heard a lot of those, Comrade. Let's go outside. The moon looks wonderful."

Had it been another day, Vinod would have ridiculed Lalita's proposal calling it a counter- revolutionary bourgeoisie luxury or would have explained to her the in-depth tactics and principles of Lenin's coup d' art. Today what he genuinely longed for was indeed the night's cool and tranquil atmosphere after a whole day's relentless, hard toil.

Vinod said: "let's go."

They had walked a long way leaving the city far behind; the city kept glimmering like a piece of half-burnt wood in Earth's crematory ground. Before them, there was the vast expanse of the uneven field, the ticklish fickleness of the moonlight.

After walking for some distance, Vinod and Lalita

both sat tiredly on a hump of the soil. Vinod initiated a boring and monotonous discussion by talking about the content of Marx's letter to Engel. Words kept bouncing in his mouth like parched rice on the frying pot.

Lalita asked with an abrupt tone of sarcasm: "Hey Vinod! Has Marx not said something about such a beautiful, cool moonlight somewhere in his writing?"

Vinod kept pondering over an answer to this question when they could hear the magic symphony of somebody's flute coming floating towards them like a wave in that sea of moonlight. The symphony mingled into the night spread all over the uneven field like a dark, furry blanket. They were all becoming one. Lalita and Vinod listened to that music like two hypnotized beings.

Within no time, they could see the faint silhouettes of two human beings coming closer and settling onto a hump of soil at a distance. There was no stopping of that flute's symphonic music. It was like a river spilling over its banks to fling itself into that sea of moonlight.

Both Lalita and Vinod were uncontrollably anxious to see those two human beings.

They came even closer.

As they approached Lalita and Vinod, the flute's music stopped. In the faint glimmer of the moonlight, Lalita and Vinod recognized them—Nayana and Kajri. They were labourers of the mill that had gone on a strike. They were from Chhotnagpur.

Their wages were stopped due to the strike. Perhaps they had to spend the night without food. Yet, they were full of life's unlimited exuberance.

Lalita said: "You play the flute so beautifully, Nayana".

Nayana answered in her Chhatisgadi[46] dialect: "Yes sister! When the moon rises over our area, we start roaming in the hills and jungles throughout the night."

The night was getting pithier and darker. Lalita and Vinod returned to their office.

Lalita kept thinking that the failure of Marxism lies here. Life is not all about a frugal calculation of production and distribution. Full wage and full belly may be its ineluctable necessity, but not its ultimate goal. Then for whom are meant this luxury of the moonlight and the fullness of Nature? Life is more beautiful than the mere, senseless act of living.

In the struggle and hullaballoo of the needy populace, Marxism had forgotten the aesthetic beauty of Nature.

Lalita said: "Vinod! Look at these two labour-class ladies. They are so full of life and vitality."

Vinod jerked and then, looked at Lalita. He felt as if somebody hit him hard on the locked door of his heart, with a bang. Nayana started playing her flute again. The fragrance of the Hina[47] flower in Kajri's wig got into his nostril like a scented fume in that moonlit night.

Vinod lifted his eyes and looked at Lalita.

Drenched in the incandescent shower of moonlight, Lalita's body sparkled with an unforeseen resplendence.

46 -A dialect spoken in Chhatishgarh, Madhya Pradesh.
47 - A sweet-smelling sub-continental flower whose botanical name is Lawsonia Inermis.

Vinod looked at her again with a feeling of extreme keenness. But the next moment he thought it was all nothing but a lavish but meaningless bourgeoisie sentiment.

Nayana and Kajri were also coming back though the same uneven field.

Lalita had to go back to her room and write tomorrow's bulletin. Her body and mind became intoxicated with a feeling of exhaustion and irritation.

The music of Nayana's flute was progressively getting dissolved in the night's brooding tranquillity.

It seemed to Lalita that the receding music was nothing but a wakeup call to Marxism and its theoretical propositions for the struggle for existence.

******

The Capital City

The alarm bell rang like someone's shout: "Get up! It's seven in the morning . . ." Another day resumed. Subodh was always afraid of the day's beginning as it was going to be horribly taxing, without any doubt. He stopped the clock's lever bearing an overt expression of irritation on his petulant, swollen face. He wished it rang after fifteen minutes.

The morning light had not yet reached the room tearing the thick, velvety veil of the night. Everything was a conglomerate mixture of shades, of liquid darkness and faintly glimmering light; Subodh stayed immersed, for the time being, in this little, kaleidoscopic fiesta of colours. On the table, the flower vase looked like a cluster of crumpled dreams. Subodh did not feel like sleeping anymore. He pressed the calling bell on the table for bed tea and the morning newspaper.

These two addictions were his morning needs. He required tea to reactivate his incapacitated and hibernating nerves. And he required the morning newspaper to involve in a clumsy mess of nonsense: whether our nation is able to produce aluminium as per its requirement or not, what the president of the United States of America told in the banquet-meeting, how many children are dying in Congo every day due to malnutrition, how fresh our prime minister looked yesterday morning, what are the chances of war with our neighbouring countries etc. These might have been questions relating to his professional life; but for him, these were futile and meaningless things in life. "Your profession burdens your life; but your life does not control your profession. This formula between your life and your profession is the real tragedy." Subodh told himself and continued: "I wish I looked into the matters of my kith and kin rather than looking into those in my surroundings. Today's newspaper is all about the life and the activities of industrialists, underworld dons, a few self-styled monks, cricket players and film superstars. These news items do not encompass the pains, pleasures and vagaries of life. There is intoxication in them."

But this was Subodh's profession . . . He was a special correspondent of a famous daily newspaper of the capital city.

Most of his time was spent in press conferences, in five-star hotels in the midst of freely offered lunches, coffees and dinners by various government as well as private agencies and organizations. And in between all these, he kept typing his report in his typewriter, willy-nilly, with a stoic and abysmal indifference.

But Subodh jovially called these invitations meal-tickets and termed these conferences free lunch sessions; his funny nomenclatures, of course, were imbued with clandestine notes of humour and sarcasm. Fascinatingly, however, there was a lot of competition amongst his friends and colleagues for these meal tickets.

Recently, there was a mammoth congregation of a few national leaders in the capital city. Amongst them, someone was a democratically elected leader; someone was a dictator and someone was a ruler whose rule might have ended anytime, through a military coup and another group might usurp power. The media reporters danced to their strange, bizarre and inexplicable tunes and projected them as national leaders of tremendous global relevance and significance.

These so-called global, national leaders were all cordially invited to the capital city to establish peace and harmony in the world. It was believed that even though they did not possess money, arms and ammunitions; they certainly had a collective voice that could create an impeccable, cosmopolitan impact.

Subodh was in no way interested in this congregation and thought that it was better to see a cricket match on TV rather than listening to these national leaders and applauding their dresses, their cuisine, their style etc. on the close circuit TVs in the media centre.

The editor however was a little annoyed with Subodh's characteristic and quintessential nihilism and told: "It's a mammoth and career-changing assignment, Subodh. There is a lot of hue and cry over it, amongst the public, and the ever-wakeful intelligentsia. How can you be so cynical and reluctant about an event of such magnitude, of such global significance and grandeur? I am surprised."

Subodh answered: "There is no novelty and innovation in these assignments, Sir. And thus, they don't attract me, at all. As simple as that!"

"What do you mean?" Said the editor, leaving a

mouthful of curly smoke into the air from his pipe. "This will be one of our biggest achievements as hosts."

Subodh answered back: "Sir! This country has seen so many farces like this. This is another one. Nothing new in this!"

The editor said in an irritated gesture: "You are an incorrigible cynic, Subodh! You always see the opposite and pessimistic side of things."

Of course, this allegation on Subodh on the editor's part was not entirely unfounded. If he could accept everything with an easy-going contentedness, he would have attained peace and happiness in life. But his life was full of a flurry of adversities, hardships and complications right from the beginning; nothing came to him with ease and effortlessness. He had seen life's ugly face from close quarters and his bitter experiences had snowballed into a strange and bizarre mental derangement, an incurable psychosis. He had presumably inherited it from his forefathers. A sinful attitude indeed!

Subodh further told the editor: "Sir! My cynicism has always helped you to comprehend things better, to estimate things more correctly."

But for his quintessential cynicism, he had become a repulsive and loathsome alien in his journalist community. One relished being safe and protected inside a congregation and there was pain and suffering in aloofness, in standing alone on the top of a mountain and looking vacantly into the silence of the valley with the sombre and dismal eye of a cynic. But Subodh perhaps relished being alone.

Finally, this global conference came to an end. Subodh's reporting was widely acclaimed and extensively admired, not only across the journalistic brotherhood, but also from various quarters of the intelligentsia who particularly relished perusing through Subodh's reported news items. Even a press-attaché from the embassy's palace had profusely congratulated Subodh on his unique and efficient reporting.

Subodh had taken complete leave for one week after the conference. Today was the last day of his leave.

He took a few sips from the cup and stroked, absentmindedly, his long and curly strips of hair with his own hand; he did it to break his sleep.

An engagement pad lied open near the bed-lamp close to the teapoy.

This capital was the city of multiple events—a symposium on poverty to be inaugurated by a minister at 11 am in the convention hall of the five-star hotel Vikramaditya, a dinner party in the moonlight club, the birth day party of Santa Saxsena etc. A man without proper dresses and etiquettes had no place here. But Subodh only knew how hollow and picayune from the core was this elegant, flashy and catchpenny elite culture? But still one had to succumb to such sophisticated requirements of high society and to gleefully entertain its grandiloquent and magnanimous show of falsity, its glittery, falsifying facade. Otherwise, what was the requirement for him sending an ornate and glitzy flower bouquet along with birthday wishes to Santa Saxena? Subodh promptly dialled a telephone number in Hotel *Blue Diamond*, ordered for a staggeringly spectacular bouquet of orchids and roses and sent it to Santa Saxena's room. Then he spoke to her and wished her a very very happy birthday. Subodh imagined, sensuously, that she was holding the bouquet in her hands and caressing the orchid and rose-clusters against her cheek and saying in a sleepy and languid voice: "How lovely! How lovely!"

The paralysed Mr. Saxena looked at Santa while squatting--helpless and incapacitated--on his wheel chair and told: "The bouquet looks fabulous. Only a lovely lady like you should own it." And then there was a little, incandescent flicker of a smile on his face.

Mrs. Saxena kissed her husband on his forehead and said: "O! How naughty you are!"

But was there an arresting, sensuous ecstasy in that kiss? A heartfelt intimacy in that embrace? Was there an unquenched thirst of ages in those apparently amorous moments of togetherness? Clearly, now it was not possible between them primarily because of their huge age-gap and also for Mr. Saxena's paralysed body's irretrievable decrepitude. Santa, though approaching forty, still looked young, dashing and refreshing. Mr. Saxena had once published an advertisement in the newspaper for a companion because he had become alone and depressed after his wife's premature death. Santa had carefully studied all the information regarding how much of share Mr. Saxena held in big companies, how huge was his bank balance, and how many palatial mansions he owned in different metropolitan cities. The companionship ended in marriage.

That day Santa had come out her palatial mansion in a certain pretext and Subodh had by chance confronted her inside a coffee house.

Subodh asked her in a carefully crafted, sentimental tone: "Santa! Are you really happy with this marriage, with this seemingly mismatching conjugal life?"

Santa took out a cigarette from her vanity bag,

lighted it and said while smoking the cigar: "Nobody is perfectly happy in this world under any circumstance, Subodh. It is only money and profitability that matters, and matters most. That is the unscripted law of our sublunary existence. Mental peace and happiness are only futile, irrelevant, old-age words."

Subodh did not enquire further, being fully aware of the discomfiting sensitivity of the matter. Santa's previous husband had divorced her. She also had legion, miscellaneous material needs and expectations. Mr. Saxena was also leading a very lonely and deserted life.

But why did Subodh need to poke his head into Santa's private matters, unwarrantedly? A lot of women like her had entered into his life like multi-coloured rainbows and had gone out like perennially shifting, vacillating clouds in the sky.

Santa would also go like them.

The telephone rang. Someone asked in an authoritative voice: "Is it Subodh Kapoor speaking?"

There was a spotted a frown of irritation on his face, surging like a gigantic hillock of wave in a convalescing sea. Again, this boring character! The voice on phone said: "Hello Subodh! This is Professor Dr. Malhotra speaking."

Subodh answered in a clandestinely irritated voice: "What's the news?"

Professor Dr. Malhotra! It was all a hoax. This Malhotra was a mere lecturer in a private college once. Now he calls himself Professor Dr. Malhotra. In this capital city, who cares for in which subject you have completed your Ph. D.? What was your thesis?

Malhotra was a huge hoax. But in today's politics riddled with tawdry show-business and nepotism, these hoaxes topped the list of successful people in the society.

Prof. Dr. Malhotra said: "Subodh! We sat together once a few days back. Let's sit today again. I have a nice thing for you."

Subodh did understand what was the meaning of a nice thing? A nice thing meant sophisticated foreign liquor. Dr. Malhotra was the union president of the fourth-class employees of the foreign embassy. Through them, he could arrange such 'nice things' quite conveniently, that too without any cost.

But the real danger that lied in accepting his invitation was that at the end of the drink he would prod you to send a report on something to the newspaper and then, publish it. A fabricated eulogy on the foreign minister, for instance! And then he would say: "The foreign minister is visiting the United Sates this weekend. This statement should be highlighted in the newspaper before his departure." And after finishing off four pegs of whiskey offered by him for free, one could hardly refute his request. Like a letterhead company, Professor Malhotra was a celebrated leader possessing the prowess to influence even the fourth wall of democracy—the media. Sometimes he could even send you in a foreign visit either in a friendship-association or in some high-level delegation. He was either the president or the secretary of half-a-dozen friendship-associations.

But Professor Malhotra and a few more like him never understood how meanly and condescendingly the foreign diplomats of the embassy looked down on them for their cheap and sleazy priggishness for free scotch and whiskey. They thought that these people could be easily bought and sold for a few bottles of whiskey; for them, these were no more than ignominious herds of purchasable and sellable commodities. And they could shamelessly lobby for their own interests through these conveniently merchandisable people. Theses sycophants were flooded everywhere . . . from the embassy to the parliament.

Sycophancy and nepotism were the fundamental principles of the capital city's politics. The bigger a sycophant you were, the more successful a politician you could be.

Professor Malhotra asked on the telephone: "Why do you keep quiet Subodh?"

"We will sit together another day, professor. There is an urgent engagement this evening." Said Subodh and kept the receiver down in a snappy and cantankerous manner.

After the end of today's symposium, there was still ample time left in the hand. Subodh told himself: "I can go a little late to Santa's dinner party tonight and spend that time sipping whiskey in Professor Malhotra's house. But he was also overawed by the latter's agonizingly oily and casuistic behaviour, that at times looked awkward and terribly inconvenient.

Pretension and deception were the ingrained, mental features of the city politicians. They pretended about the greatness of their leadership qualities in the newspapers. That was their satisfaction.

This Professor Malhotra was an unabashed creature, to put it straight. To give attendance in the embassy was his everyday business, though it was not always possible for him to move inside and meet the diplomat. But once upon a time he had some sort of closeness with him. The latter once told him, perhaps out of a friendly goodwill-gesture, that he can go a long way in life. Capitalising on that, Professor Malhotra declared outside, overwhelmed by a mirthful and dreamy exuberance, that he is an important person of the embassy. He also declared in his friend-circle that the honourable diplomat intends to make him the corporator of a big city. The news also reached the other sycophants surrounding the diplomat for some personal benefits and for their long-cherished dreams to be fulfilled. They got envious and tried very tactfully to instigate him against the professor. On one occasion when Professor Malhotra was coming out of the palace after presenting a flower bouquet to the diplomat, one of the latter's acolytes told him point blank on his face, in a very clear and unambiguous voice: "Mr. Professor! People in the palace are not particularly liking your regular and unsolicited entry into the embassy. It's better if you come less frequently to the palace." Professor Malhotra immediately understood the gesture behind such words and gradually, his entry into the embassy was getting restricted. And it did not take him long to understand that the real diktat was indeed from the diplomat himself, in a clandestine and surreptitiously implicative manner though, for he never told things directly to anybody on his face. He always passed the information to the targeted person through his acolytes. Even Prof. Malhotra was also doing this job in the past. So, he could understand the implications even better.

These days, he stands beneath a mango tree inside the palace and welcomes the visitors with benign, folded hands. While he welcomes them, one could readily spot on his face the serene and assuaged smile of Lord Buddha and while greeting the people, he lifts his right hand in a benevolent posture, as if to bless his devotees like the Lord himself. Amongst the visitors are usually the rich people, businessmen and industrialists from different places and everybody who comes inside the embassy knows Prof. Malhotra, in some way or other. And Professor Malhotra tells them: "You please go inside and meet the diplomat. I am always at your service."

Self-aggrandisement in the media is an essential survival-tactic for people like Professor Malhotra. But for that, of course, they have to arrange a lot of good things (branded liquor) for the journalists. But of course, it is not a big thing for the president of the fourth-class employees of the embassy to smuggle a few branded liquor bottles outside the embassy. Professor Malhotra was adept in this business. Even his biggest enemies would accept it, unequivocally.

But it was also becoming increasingly irritating for Subodh to publish Professor Malhotra's statements in the newspaper for a few pegs of whiskey, a chancellor cigarette-packet and a cheaply offered dinner. But Professor Malhotra was in no mood to leave Subodh. He telephoned him again: "Subodh! If you do not come, the evening will be spoiled." Subodh answered with clenched teeth and with a succinct expression of cantankerousness on his face: "Sorry! Thanks."

No! He also did not want to go to Devinder Singh's breakfast anymore. This Devinder Singh is also another notoriously cunning character in the capital city. He is a sub-agent in a European military aircraft manufacturing company. A lobby is always required for selling aircrafts and for a lobby, one requires clandestine, negative advertisement against other competing aircraft manufacturing companies. And for this, one needs the cooperation of many—starting from parliament members to the journalists. And that is why it was a regular thing for Subodh to get invited to breakfasts, lunches or dinners into Devinder Singh's Jorbag palace. But slowly he had started disliking this business of sycophancy. He telephoned Devinder Singh and gently apologized for not being able to attend his breakfast invitation.

Then he got busy preparing for a symposium on poverty in Hotel Vikramaditya.

If his vehicle's carburettor did not trouble him, Subodh could have reached the symposium in time. But when he entered the hall after checking in at the reception counter, only a few minutes of the esteemed leader's speech had passed. The audience applauded his talk with passionate and vigorous clappings. Perhaps the great leader had delivered an extremely valuable harangue.

After the leader's speech was over, a costly safari-suit-clad gentleman climbed onto the stage, eliciting a phrenic and highbrowed demeanour. He stood on the stage in a dramatic posture, threw back a few braids of hairs from his forehead and started defining poverty: "If poverty is not correctly defined right at the outset, then all endeavours for its removal would be tantamount to swimming through condensed fog. All these ardent brainstormings would go in vain if the very word 'poverty' is not correctly defined. A high-level committee must be constituted to first define poverty, correctly." Then the gentleman went on . . .

A huge and rambunctious round of applause from the audience filled the thin air of the hall; the gentleman mistook it as an emotional response from the audience as an appreciation of his talk. Even the esteemed leader greeted him with a benevolent smile. However, the gentleman failed to understand that the audience's clapping was a purely a customary thing, a mere reflex action. They clapped for every talker.

The second speaker looked like a congenital rebel—Professor Roshan Lal. A very well-known face in the leftist, intellectual circle! He was a faculty of Sociology in a very reputed educational institution dominated by leftist orientations. He wore a thick 'khaddar' trouser and Punjabi and a pair of thick-framed, zero-power spectacles on his eyes. From his shoulders, hung a 'khaddar-cloth-made' Santi-Niketan-bag. A beard on his chin along with a few deepening frowns ravaging across his forehead attributed to him the precious and sophisticated look of an intellectual. Professor Lal took out his thesis from his bag and again kept it inside and then, started his speech in a slow and calculated voice which however turned fiery and vigorous within moments like blazing lava emanating from a volcano: "Whatever the previous speaker said is nothing but the repetitions of the voices of the capitalists, of the multinational company owners." The essence of Professor Lal's speech was that unless these exploitative capitalists were removed from this nation, poverty alleviation could never be achieved; it would rather go on increasing. Another uproarious round of applause filled the hall's exited and intellectualized air.

Now it was ten minutes to one o' clock.

Everybody was busy with lunch.

It was 3 o' clock and the lunch was over—a lunch that had five courses of different items.

In the afternoon session, came to speak Professor Lakdiwala—noted Gandhian economist. He was also outrageously opposed to the nation's capitalists, but for a different reason though. In his opinion, the only route to poverty-alleviation was the adoption of village-economy and promotion of small-scale industries. For him, the nation required no power plants. Cow-dung-gas would suffice. As long as there was 'charkha[48],' what was the need of a textile plant? Gandhiji of course had gone up to a single stitching machine. Not more than that! Of course, looking at the vastness of the nation, one might need trains and aeroplanes. But why would one need these sophisticated things in a competition-less village economy?

Professor Lakdiwala, keeping in tune with his communist ideology, wore a pair of motor-tyre-made shoes, a 'khaddar' dhoti that ran feverishly up to his knees, a half-shirt, a long beard below his chin and a pair of thick-framed looking glasses on his eyes. He was completely bald-headed, but never hesitated to speak and act in exaggerated and melodramatic manners whenever necessary. He spoke his mind without any inhibition. He started his speech:

"Poverty is nothing but a 'thinking.' It has nothing to do with economy. You won't find a village in our country from where a guest will come back in empty stomach. Families, who cannot afford to eat meal twice a day, will also arrange a meal for the guest. Such mental richness makes them survive in the midst of this circumambient, cataclysm of poverty. So, poverty can never be alleviated without inculcating in the public's mind a profound sense of mental richness. Otherwise they will remain both poverty-stricken and mentally impoverished."

Prof. Lakdiwala went on and on . . .

---

48   -An indigenous, wooden tool to weave clothes. It was used by the father of the nation Mahatma Gandhi to do the same.

But perhaps his speech did not touch anybody's sentiment. After his speech got over, of course, one or two people gave a few customary claps, willy-nilly. But it was also an indication of the fact that many people, who did not clap, did not agree to his ideas.

The participants looked at their watches in worried and fidgety gestures. After devouring heavy, sumptuous meals, they did not have the patience to listen to another boring speech on poverty.

Subodh also did not have that patience. He came out of the discussion hall. For him, it was all sheer wastage of time and a fake, concocted show of intellectuality.

He typed the report in the newspaper room in the evening. In his report, he duly highlighted the ingenuous statements of Professor Lakdiwala; but his writing was in fact an acute and fierce criticism of such fake, phony and counterfeit facades going on in the nation in the name of intellectualizing poverty. However, the news editor put huge red and blue cross-marks on his writing and admonished him: "Mr. Subodh! If you continue to write like this, acerbically, then you will be very soon fired by your boss. So be careful in future."

Subodh answered: "He is most welcome to do that, Sir."

Outside, the evening had grown dense and pithy. Steeped in gas-light, the roads looked colourful and different. Subodh did not feel like going back to his flat; he dressed himself up for Santa Acharya's birthday party. Before driving to Santa's place, he parked his car outside a garden and went inside to sleep flat on its grassy lawn and to kill the day's boredom by looking vacuously at the starry night sky. He ran his fingers through his greyish hair and told himself: "Even this will do."

At least there was no faking in the evening's slow, intoxicating wind and in the night's caliginous darkness.

While driving his car into the golden premises of No. 3 Moonlight Colony, Subodh felt had he not reached in a wrong address? No-This was No. 3 Moonlight Colony. He was well-acquainted with that place. To clear his doubts, he stopped his vehicle in the midway and looked at the roadside Eucalyptus trees. No! He had not made any mistake. Today was Santa Saxena's birthday party. Below the portico was parked her imported Limousine car and no other vehicle or human 'being' was visible inside that huge, sepulchral premise. The big compound and the duplex looked morbidly empty and mournfully sombre. The bright halogens outside the glass windows and doors had exacerbated the tranquillity of the surrounding.

"But where has everybody gone?" Subodh asked himself.

While coming out of his car in a disturbed, lackadaisical manner, he met a uniform-wearing servant on the veranda. The servant saluted him.

Subodh asked: "What is the matter? Why others have not arrived yet?"

The servant answered: "The invitation was at 8.30, Sir."

Subodh looked at his wrist watch and was surprised to find that it had stopped at 8.30. Something had gone wrong with it.

He was a little dejected and despondent that he had

missed the party. To relieve his mental agony and tension, the servant told him in a softened voice: "Sir, Please go to the drawing room inside. Sir (Santa's husband) is resting there."

There was no use going back. Subodh went inside. The drawing room looked piteously empty and enervated. Another servant was cleaning the sofa and the centrepieces with a broom. Another one was busy embellishing the flower vases with different-shaped flowers. Subodh, of course, was not at all an unfamiliar figure in this place. The servants greeted him with salutes and requested him to sit comfortably inside the room.

But Subodh was very restless. He asked: "Where is madam?"

He knew he could meet Santa another day in some gathering in a party somewhere. But if he meets her today alone on the occasions of her birthday in this tranquil, captivating moment, he would definitely take her by a pleasant surprise. There was excitement in giving her such surprises.

Someone said: "Madam is inside her bedroom."

Today Subodh wanted to give a surprise to Santa as if it would have been the most precious gift for her on her birthday. He walked stealthily, like a clandestine leopard, on the carpeted stairs towards Santa's bedroom on the upper storey.

Santa had not bolted the door from inside. The light inside the room was sparsely visible through the thin fissures between the door and the door screen. Subodh's flagrant eyes lit up with naughtiness. He thought Santa would be ecstatic to see him alone near her after such a long time. He lifted the curtain slightly from outside and peeped inside the room.

Santa sat languidly on a small mahogany chair in front of her glitzy and sumptuous dressing mirror. She looked lost inside herself, narcissistically. Seemingly enamoured by her own reflected image in the mirror, she had perhaps forgotten the situational immediacy of her environment. She looked frozen to stillness just like the frigid and fragrant cosmetic bottles and boxes, languorously placed on the dressing table. It looked as if she was acquiescently hypnotized by her own image on the mirror.

Before taking a new make-up, Santa had gotten herself rid of all the previous make-ups. Beneath the new make-up, nevertheless, lay concealed the many vermiculate wrinkles on her face, the many abrasive scars of her growing age, the many grotesque frowns beneath her two sunken eyes and finally, the growing, repellent, ugliness of her dwindling youth.

It was a horribly putrid and sickening revelation for Subodh to see Santa without make-up. Her bob-cut hair was the envy of many women; it was an object of attraction and adoration for her male friends like Subodh; it was the insignia of her glowing youth and beauty. But O God! What was this? It was a dull, pestilential wig. Subodh could not believe his eyes. The wig lay abandoned on the gaudy and shimmering dressing table like a dead thing.

Santa had already become bald-headed. The baldness of her head glimmered unsavourily in the dimly ocular efflux of pinkish, rubicund electric light in the room. Some scattered locks of her clammy, caliginous hair hanged dishevelled from her head. She looked like a ghost, a gruesome apparition of an ugly and obscene silhouette in the dark. Even her curvy eyebrows looked fake and feverishly artificial. She had decorated them with her hands.

Subodh stealthily walked down the stairs. It looked as if he had no strength in his feet, neither did he have the old excitement to join Santa's birthday party.

It seemed to him as if Santa Saxena was the true insignia of the capital city's pretensions.

*****

Vagabond

I

A thorough gentleman! He has a handsome monthly earning and has a decent family life with his wife and son. His bank balance has increased of late; but along with it has also increased his body fat. And along with them have also come dyspepsia, diabetes and blood pressure. This family life has given him pleasure. Oh! . . . While shaving, his blade slipped off. Kamal started bleeding. Oh! This growing age gives nothing but pain; it gives you death every moment. Kamal bled from his chin.

He took out his handkerchief to wipe off the blood. The silken handkerchief emitted the fragrance of 'evening-in-Paris' perfume. Mallika told she will come today. Kamal, half-shaved, got up, went to the door and locked it from outside. He lifted the half-broken railing of the window and came back into the room, and washed his face with soap. Then he emitted a long, deep sigh of relief. It was a beautiful idea. He could always lock the room from outside and sleep inside, peacefully. By doing so, he could fully avoid the nagging and cantankerous house-owner, the noisy and vociferous mixture-seller, and of course, Mallika; they would think that Kamal is absent as the room is locked from outside. Kamal lifted the half-broken window's rusty, fuliginous railings and came into the room, and washed his face

with soap. Then he emitted a long, deep sigh of relief. It was a wonderful idea; he could always lock the room from outside and sleep in his room, peacefully.

*****

Kamal travelled back in time through the memory lane.

That day Mallika was sleeping on his chest in the secluded corner of a park. Kamal said: "Mallika! I don't believe in love. A man does not have emotions; he does not have sentiments; he does not have soft feelings. He believes only in one basic, primitive instinct--lustfulness. Love is his incarceration; marriage is a confinement. But woman needs love. For that, she needs a man. That's why she loves her man and loves him more than her life. But for a man love is nothing but unconditional surrender. And I hate surrender, Mallika. I hate surrender."

Mallika said; "You are a cruel man, Kamal! You are a cruel man. You know Kamal! How much I have suffered by falling in love with you? Can you imagine what terrible pain and agony I have undergone in getting enmeshed with an unemotional, vagabond like you?"

Mallika's gown was full of the 'bloomed-lotus' embroidery.

She was a sub-inspector in the Police Department. She was chubby, dusky-complexioned, big-toothed.

*****

Nine o' clock in the morning! On a plane sheet of paper, Kamal scribbled the whole day's routine--willy-nilly, absentmindedly. He had to catch hold of that rascal Basant first.

Kamal took out a cigarette from the ash tray and lighted it.

He met Basant and they engaged in a coquettish, friendly conversation. Kamal said; "Basant! You are not only stupid, you are a big moron. Hey idiot! You were giving singing-tuition to some students and were earning something, and that was your earning for the whole month. Now you have left that. Then how would you manage your expenses?"

Basant said: "O! That is true. I had not yet thought of it. But Kamal! If there is no vigour of life here, then how can there be music? Why are these girls learning music? Sometimes I feel like getting asphyxiated before these girls. Ok . . . Can you lend me twenty rupees? The house owner is a monster. He has confiscated my harmonium. Now he eyes on my table."

Basant threw his long hair towards the back of his head.

*****

It has been six months since then. There was no news of Mr. Basant. Gone were also those twenty rupees.

Kamal said to himself: "Today I have to catch hold of the other fellow, Sripati Babu. Sripati Chaudhury! Lake Road! What is today's date? Monday! In which nostril I am breathing right now? Left nostril! Breathing in the left nostril on Monday! It's a positive premonition. Hey Mother

Kali! Hey Mother Shyama! I wish Sripati Chaudhury does a life insurance policy with me today. I heard he is ready for an insurance policy of one lakh rupees. I will enjoy its commission for the whole year. Oh God! This coat has lost its iron and has become wrinkled. But it's still manageable. But where is Mallika? The ugly Mallika? Ugly both in body and mind! But what is the harm in marrying her? It does not matter even if she has a hundred affairs. Still she has a body that can be enjoyed. Her body is good enough."

It was already eleven. No! There was no news of Mallika. Kamal wiped off his face with a handkerchief. The fragrance of the 'evening-in-Paris' perfume was right in his nostrils.

II

Oh shit! Kamal hit a boulder. His boot-sole cracked at the right corner. This rascal road-corporation! The whole road is full of boulders and potholes. Nobody bothers if half of your foot goes. You will get some iodine and some cotton from the nearby dispensary and your injury will slowly heal. But at least eight rupees will be required to repair this cracked sole. It's actually the cost of a cigarette packet. It also means ten tension-free dreamy moments. Or else, four cups of special tea!

The next street is the fish-market-street. Then there is the Broadway Restaurant.

Below the coat, there was a monstrous beast gnawing the inner walls of his stomach with its sharpened nails. Hunger!

Kamal said to himself: "I need a cup of tea. Yes!

Only one cup of tea! My nerves have become dormant. One cup of tea is five rupees. One pack of cigarette is ten rupees. The bus fare is twenty rupees. But I have only ten rupees in my pocket. It's better to walk to Sripati Chaudhury's on foot."

Kamal started walking.

III

A big road! Some cobbler was calling: "Shoe-polish Sir! Shoe polish! Don't you need shoe-polish, Sir? Don't you need it? Your sole is cracked sir. Your sole is cracked. Your right finger is visible through the crack, Sir."

Kamal kept on walking heedlessly. After a few steps there will be the fish market.

He reached the number 3 fish market. But where was Mr. Basant Das? The door was locked. On a bench at a distance was squatting the pea-seller Mr. Khan while sipping tea from a cup, intermittently. "Perhaps he is also waiting for Basant. Oh God! I won't be able to meet this bloody fugitive Basant. The rascal has escaped." Kamal said to himself.

"Then I must meet Sripati Chaudhury. But again, his house is four miles away." Thought Kamal.

"Oh! Here comes Basant's house owner. He can give me some information about him." Kamal said to himself.

Basant's house owner greeted Kamal with a ceremonious hello and said: "Good evening Kamal Babu. Look at this Basant Babu. A thorough gentlemen! But see! He has not paid my house rent for months together."

Kamal answered: "Where is Basant Babu? I am also searching for him."

The house owner answered: "He has absconded. I have confiscated his harmonium from him. Now he has vanished after throwing his table in a corner of my house. He told me he is getting married and he will clear all my rents after marriage."

"Basant's marriage? When is he getting married? That day Mallika was also telling about a marriage." Kamal asked himself with a clear note of surprise.

*****

That day Mallika told Kamal: "Kamal! We will build our dream-home away from the clattery and dismaying din and bustle of the city. You and me, a small house, a greenery-filled hill at the back and a swiftly streaming river in the front, smiling at us all the time!" On another evening also, Mallika came to Kamal with the same marriage proposal, with the same boring, monotonous dream-talk.

Kamal told her with an intention to hurt: "Mallika! How many dream-homes have you constructed with other men before me?"

Mallika kept mum while smiling impishly turning her face away.

This Mallika is a strange creature. She can easily take any offence with a smiling face. She has forgotten her past; now she wants a family even at the cost of pain, humiliation and suffering.

That day Mallika's wig was decorated with beautiful red flowers. Red flowers on a black wig...

Mallika told while answering to Kamal's questions;

"Kamal! Body and soul are two different things. I have looked for that soul in many bodies. But today, I have lost the beauty of this body at the age of thirty-five. What attraction will you find in this worn-out body of mine? But today I have come with the attraction of the soul."

There was the sweet and beautiful fragrance of the 'evening-in-Paris' perfume emanating from Mallika's scented body.

Kamal said: "Mallika! You and I are now far away from the din and bustle of the main town, in a tranquil bamboo-covered village. On all sides, there are sprawling green fields merging into the sky at the distant horizon. Let's enjoy the beauty of Nature."

Mallika left after some time.

Kamal said to himself: "There is a peace in this surrender. There is no shame, no torture, no humiliation in self-protection. Basant has taken the right track. Nobody can escape from the society. There is no point fighting with the opposite sex for nothing. There is absolute peace and bliss in this resistance-less, surrender. This fight is meaningless. Om Shanti! Shanti! Shanti! This is wasteland . . . Above is the sprawling, blue firmament of the sky."

IV

A little distance away!

After taking a right turn from the Motiganj Street, there was the flashy and elegant 'Chaudhury Mansions.' Sripati Chaudhury's Mansions! The blessed son of destiny! He can make an insurance of at least one lakh rupees. Kamal offered him a cigarette. Mr. Chaudhury said: "No thanks!"

While trying to persuade him for the insurance, Kamal said: "See Mr. Chaudhury! Great poet Bharati has said: "Nalini Dalagata Jalamati Taralang (Life is like a tiny water droplet on a lotus leaf)." Bharati? Or Magha? Or Bana? Or Kalidasa? Or Shankaracharya? Kamal could not recollect. But he continued; "You must have heard Mr. Chaudhury that in America, the girls insure even the moles on their cheeks. Even the hair on their heads!" Kamal's voice looked convincing and persuasive though Mr. Chaudhury did not look very convinced and left bidding Kamal a sharply stinging adieu.

Kamal left the Chaudhury mansions, put a cigarette in his mouth and lighted it to rejuvenate his gruelling body and mind. The prolonged dusk of the last spring! There were rows of Deodar[49] trees on both sides of Lake Road. It looked as if the whole world was sleeping. There was no street vendor, no 'shoe-polish-shouting' cobbler, no noise. Only, small piles of fallen Deodar leaves all along! Here there is no obstacle, no pothole. . . . Here, the motion of the universe is smooth and uncomplicated. A motor cycle raced past Kamal. The Deodar leaves flew into the air for a moment and then fell scattered on the ground like slain soldiers in a battlefield.

Kamal tried his luck another day. There was the huge 'Chaudhury Mansions' right in front. A Ghurkha[50] durwan[51] dozed near the gate like a tranquilized bear. Kamal stretched his coat with his hands to make it look ironed. The horn of a locomotive motor vehicle was heard from inside. The Ghurkha durwan got up from his sleep with a jerk and squeezed a bamboo stick beneath his

49   A thin-sub-continental tree with long flowers.
50   A Nepali and Indian tribe.
51   Indian colloquial term for watchman.

shoulder, stood up and saluted to the man sitting inside the car and then, opened the iron-gate. A gigantic black-coloured car went out and raced into the distant horizon. Left behind were clusters of spiralling smoke emitted from its silencer-pipe, small whirlpools of reddish dust from the road and a bunch of dry, desiccated Deodar leaves fallen from the trees.

"What do you want?" Asked the Ghurkha durwan to Kamal while squatting on his chair. The irritation was visible on his face for his sleep was disturbed.

Kamal told in a slow voice with clenched teeth: "I want your head." The durwan obviously did not hear it. While lighting a half-burnt 'bidi[52],' he said: "Sahib just went out. You cannot meet him today."

Kamal felt like smacking the durwan on his dilated nose.

V

Again a long, stretching road of five miles back! Kamal's legs were paining. He had to go back and give it another try the next day. There were only ten rupees left in his pocket. Of course, he had to come by bus the next day. The bus fare would be twenty rupees.

Someone threw a lot of ground-nut-chaffs on him from above. In the approaching darkness of the evening, Kamal looked at the man sitting on the wall nearby. Someone was happily chewing ground nuts sitting on that wall. Kamal felt like dragging that man's feet and then,

---

52   A thin smoking pipe containing tobacco inside. It is smoked by many people who are addicted to tobacco smoke.

throwing him on the ground. In the meanwhile, the man jumped onto the ground from the wall. In the dim street light, Kamal could see that he was no other than his friend Vinod, standing in front of him in a stylish posture with a packet of ground nuts in his hand.

Kamal asked: "What were you doing on that wall Vinod?"

Vinod answered in a taunting voice: "I was performing yoga."

Kamal asked: "What do you mean?"

Vinod said: "I mean yoga. I can see past, present and future, Kamal. I know you went to meet Sripati Chaudhury to make a life insurance for him. Right? But before you have just reached his house, he went on in his Packard car for an evening ride. Right?

Kamal asked in a surprised tone: "How could you know this, man?

Vinod answered in a sympathetic voice: "Hey! I was watching it all from this wall. The moment you approached the gate of 'Chaudhury Mansions,' he went out in his car for an evening ride. I was watching it all from here. Then after getting a kick from the durwan, you are coming back with a downcast head. Isn't it right my friend? If you did not want a life insurance policy from him, then why would you have gone there? This is all sheer common sense my friend, sheer common sense. You do not need to be a rocket scientist to understand this."

Kamal asked: "But Vinod! What was the need for you to come so long from five miles away to sit on this wall and chew ground nuts?"

Vinod looked at him and smiled and then, both started walking together.

Vinod pushed the pack of ground nuts into Kamal's hand and said: "It's big, sad news bother. You know Mallika. She is a sub-inspector in the Police Department and gets a salary of two hundred rupees per month and also free lodging. A free, independent and healthy life she lives! I had proposed her to marry me. Let her be above thirty-five! Let her be ugly-looking . . ."

Kamal added: "Let her be thin-breasted, dark-complexioned, tall-toothed . . ."

Vinod said: "If I married her, all my problems would have been solved. I could have easily completed my research project on 'primitive human culture' without any financial difficulty."

Kamal asked: "But why would Mallika want to marry a 'good-for-nothing' creature like you?"

Vinod answered: "Hey idiot! This whole Earth runs on the principle of relativity. Everything is relative here. I may be a 'good-for-nothing' creature for you. But I am precious for Mallika. You know what she told me? She said: "Vinod! I have come with the beauty of my soul for you. My body has lost all its attraction at the age of thirty-five."

Kamal asked in an injured voice: "Then what? What did she say more?

Vinod said: "No! She said nothing more. I was till now hiding from her, from the ravenous appeal of her soul. But now when I have decided to marry her, I hear that she has already gotten married."

Kamal felt like falling from the sky and asked with

an anxious voice: "Mallika has gotten married! When? To whom?"

Vinod answered: "I don't know when. But I know she has married that vagabond Basant Das. He was teaching her Sitar. That is when their romance started and then, he has married her. They have left the town yesterday somewhere for honeymoon."

Kamal said to himself: "Oh God! Everything is lost. My last hope for Mallika is also gone. With that also is gone the hope of getting back my twenty rupees from that rascal Basant. Now if I ask him that money, he will answer: "That money is our marriage-gift." Then also, Kamal had already looted a lot of money from Mallika in the name of being her ardent lover. But still, he thought this might be a golden opportunity for a making a life insurance policy for Basant. He thought he will go to him and tell: "See Basant! I am telling all this to you as your well-wisher. Now you are into family life. There are lots of responsibilities in family life, but there are also possibilities of untoward mishaps. So, to keep the destiny of your family secured, you must get a life insurance for yourself."

Kamal discovered another thorn in his sole. It was now impossible for him to walk any more with his shoes on. He lifted a piece of paper from the road, wrapped it around his shoes and kept walking with naked feet.

Vinod told Kamal: "Now do you understand friend? Why I was sitting on that wall and chewing ground-nuts, far away from the din and bustle of the city? I was doing so out of pure grief and frustration. I was cursing the universe for the torture that it has inflicted on me."

But Kamal could not so easily forgive that rascal

Basant inside his mind. "Buffoon! He did not give me my twenty rupees. And again, he has also married Mallika secretly, without even informing any of us." Kamal said complainingly.

In the front, there was a restaurant.

One got very tasty prawn cutlets here. There was the beautiful fragrance of prawn cutlet in the wind. Both the friends started smelling it. Kamal carefully scrambled for money in his pocket. The cruel beast of hunger had already started gnawing his belly from inside.

Vinod placed his hand on Kamal's shoulder and said; "Come friend! We are feeling very hungry."

Both of them got into the restaurant without wasting further time. First Vinod, then Kamal! Both sat near a table in the corner.

Vinod hit the table in his hand and called the restaurant-boy in a heavy voice: "Boy! Boy!"

Kamal said in a timid voice: "There is not a single rupee in my pocket, friend. There is not a single coin there."

Vinod said; "It's not easy to fool me Kamal! I have heard the jingling sound of coins in your pocket. Now you see what is in my pocket."

Vinod took out the inside cloth of his two pant pockets. Some ground nuts came out from them and fell on the ground.

Kamal cursed Vinod in a cramped voice with clenched teeth—shirker, idiot, dacoit, rascal. In the name of friendship, you called me to this restaurant and now you want to rob me off the last traces of my little treasure.

By that time, the half-pant wearing restaurant-boy had already come to the table and was waiting for the orders.

Kamal told in a helpless voice: "Four prawn cutlets."

A Hindi gazal[53] played inside the restaurant. Vinod started singing keeping in tune with the song.

The restaurant-boy came back with two prawn-cutlets in each plate and placed them on the table. Vinod put one cutlet into his mouth and started chewing it like a wild animal.

VI

The friends came out of the restaurant and lighted their respective cigarettes.

Kamal asked: "What next?"

Vinod answered while leaving a mouthful of smoke into the air: "The journey is aimless and also, endless, my friend."

Kamal remembered his dilapidated rented house in that dirty slum. The house-owner must be sitting on the veranda waiting for him for the rent and would be twisting his moustache to kill time. Once this image floated in his mind, all his courage to go back to the rented house vanished into the air like smoke.

Echoing Vinod's words, Kamal told: "Truly friend! The journey is aimless."

Vinod dragged one of Kamal's arms towards one street and said: "I am very tired, friend."

---

53   A kind of Indian classical song.

Kamal asked: "But where? You cannot enter the park at 12 o' clock in the night. The police will arrest us and we have finally to spend time in the police station."

Vinod answered: "No! It's not the park. It's the refugee camp in front."

VII

The refugee camp!

Initially, it was somebody's jute 'go down.' It was a huge asbestos-covered hall where forty families had taken shelter. It was also terribly hot inside. Therefore, forty small families were sleeping outside in the field, to get the cool, soothing breeze of the evening. Forty furnaces were burning out there. One furnace for one family! Somewhere boiled rice was getting separated from the boiling water; somewhere ladies were kneading breads. Along with that, there were the sounds of babies crying, the old folks shouting and the bangles of the ladies jingling intermittently. Vinod slept on a mat folding both his hands beneath his head. Kamal also placed the coat below his head carefully for the fear of its ironing getting destroyed. Oh! It was so peaceful. The calm, soothing evening breeze! Millions of smiling stars in the sky! And the stealthily approaching darkness! From a distance was audible the din and bustle of the city.

At some distance away, a lady was kneading the bread and then, warming it in the fire.   Around her, her four siblings were looking at her like hungry puppies. In the light of that fire, her thin and scraggy face looked clearer. She looked like the living effigy of tolerance.

Vinod thought: "I have lost one relation. I need not be sad and broken. I will build another relation, another house. Man has survived through all bad lucks, all curses, and will continue to survive through them."

That lady took out one bread from the pot, made it into four parts and gave one to each of her four siblings, and then, put another bread on fire.

Vinod had started snoring.

VIII

Kamal has also slept.

You could call these people vagabonds. You could call them beggars. No issues . . .

Vinod had slept. But if he was awake, he would have gotten up and told: "I have researched into the whole of the human history from the old stone-age till today and found out that those who have not surrendered to the society and have remained aloof, have always suffered. Sadness, bad luck, humiliation and pain have been their eternal companions. But they have always searched for innovation and held to the society the light of newness. And in that light, the world has always rediscovered its identity. They may be the cursed human beings. The thin-breasted ugly Krishnas and Mallikas have come to their houses with the appeal of their souls. But these people have run away. You may call them lunatics, vagabonds."

But Vinod had always found evidence in support of these people from History.

Vinod had slept.

Kamal's snoring has become louder.

The lady has finished preparing her breads. Her four siblings had already slept.

*****

The Flood's Companion

Govind Pattanaik! An old man! With genuflected posture, he sat on the ground and kept surveying the interminable profusion of circumambient flood-water around the little, ensconced and marooned isle. The water stretched unendingly beyond his blurring vision. Two rivers "Keluni" and "Baghuni" had joined together diabolically to generate this devastating flood that befell on the riverside-dwellers like destiny's abominable curse. There were only unfathomable greyish water, brimming bubbles and murderous whirlpools gurgling and frothing viciously around the isle; it created the ghastly monstrosity of imminent death that was set to devour the frightened souls on the isle with its fiery, cavernous mouth.

These two small rivers that usually lay emptied and waterless like two dead snakes throughout the whole year, had suddenly sprung into diabolic action to become a unified flinger of death and destruction on unprotected and endangered mankind. Because of a trench in Paika Bridge, they were filled with overflowing and voluminous masses of water thereby generating flood—a flood that was so fierce and annihilating that it could even cleave a snake that came its way into two halves. The submerged villages looked like distant isles that gleamed flickeringly with sunlight in the day and moonlight in the night. There lied at a distance the submerged Nachhipur village: only the bamboo forest's hairy, tousled top was sparingly visible, and also was unobtrusively visible the 'washed-away' and 'flood-plundered' top of the mango orchard.

Yes! Once the Mangarajpur dam had collapsed like this, all on a sudden with a loud and uproarious bang, generating a sweeping overflow of water that snowballed into an ugly and devastating flood. Govinda Babu pensively scrambled through the reservoir of old memories that kept haunting his troubled psyche like a pestilential ghost, even many years after the flood's actual occurrence. A few village folks including him went floating on a roof and were finally stuck on a little isle and were saved by the benevolent and protective almighty's assuaging providence. He was twelve or thirteen by that time. Now, carrying loads of experience in his mature and ripened mind, he is well-acquainted with the gravity of a flood-scenario. Today's younger generation nevertheless does not have much understanding of the cataclysmic power of flood. They harbour a false sense of security that there is a dam at the top which would never collapse and thus, there won't be any flood. All water shall be preserved in the reservoir.

But has this infinitesimally small creature called man ever conquered the indomitable mights of water, wind and fire? Oh! The ripened corns were submerged in the ever-rising flood water. The mountain-like cornstalk was swept away in the flood. How could one stop it? It was heartrending to witness Nature's fury from such close quarters. It was all God's wish...

Phagu Rout was a school teacher. While leaving home for this small, 'protective-looking' isle, he had managed to bring with him this transistor radio that updated the flood-news every half-an-hour. One could wonder that they could exhibit more promptness in constructing dams rather than uproariously announcing flood news.

Govinda Pattanaik looked in another direction. "What shall I get from listening to that flood-news announcement? Will that mountainous mound of paddy come back? Will that gigantic pile of corn-stack come back?" He thought. Hari Dash rushed to listen to the flood-announcement: "The water level of the river is rising because of the release of eleven lakh cusecs of water from the reservoir. . ."

The transistor made a sudden, bizarre and jarring sound and stopped. "Hey! Why did you stop the transistor at the right time?" Hari Dash asked in an irritated and cacophonous voice. His nerves trembled with excitement. "When did I stop it? It's getting stopped at times due to sudden power failure." Phagu Rout said.

"O God!" Said Hari Dash. "The water level shall rise then." The waves of infernal terror rippling through Hari Dash's dazed and terrified eyes like the rising waves ravaging across the commoved surface of a convalescing sea were immensely visible. Phagu Rout intensified his fear by superimposing his frightening comments on Hari Dash's tormenting fearsomeness: "I think the water level shall rise even more. See the seething effervescence of water bubbles."

Govinda Pattanaik said: "Listen! It seems as if there is a cloudburst at the river's upper end. The thunderous uproar of the darkening clouds is audible from a distance.

Hey look on! A dark cloud hangs like an ominous, giant vulture over your head." Hari Dash had heard from his infancy that if there is cloudburst at the river's upper end, then there will be a definite, devastating flood . . .

In a panicky gesture, Hari Dash threw a timorous glance at the accumulating flood water on all sides. He repented why did he imprudently come to this Talabani isle while his village folks went onto the canal bridge, instead, with their children and livestock? Presumably, it was a relatively safer place. But the next moment, he apprehended that the rising flood water might even submerge the canal bridge, engulf it like a water-monster. He conjectured that there was a fissure in that bridge; it could grow bigger and bigger thereby proliferating and widening the existing cracks in the bridge and then, the bridge might collapse, all on a sudden, crushed into a topsy-turvy mess of cracked soil and boulders inundated in the flood-water.

Was there any guarantee that such a thing won't happen? Now the Talabani isle might also be submerged under water for the water level was ominously rising, knowing no bounds, with water-hillocks piled on water-hillocks in enormous, hoarding masses. But people said that even the severest flood had not been able to submerge this isle, thanks to its unusual height from the sea-level. But, of course, it was all unsubstantiated hearsay. Initially, there was a small palm forest on the isle, embellishing its head like dishevelled, tousled lock of hair. But the farmers slowly started cutting the palm trees and there was not even a trace of the forest now. Now the isle lied completely bare, desiccated and forlorn apart from a lone, abandoned 'neem' tree standing at the top like an antique and derelict statue. Hari Dash started climbing onto the tree fearing the rising water level; he thought that the tree would be a safe haven for him due to its height. But he fell down.

Dasa Pradhan sat a little far away. He shouted: "Hey moron! Why are you climbing onto the tree? There are three cobras lying circled on the branches. I have seen them."

"O! Snake! Snake!" It looked as if Hari Dash's eyes bulged out in insidious terror.

Jayee Mohanty suffered from chronic osteoporosis in his waist. He could not stand straight. One would wonder how he climbed onto this isle with such a deplorable health condition guiding his way through the turbulently flowing streams. It was strange and inconceivable. The irrepressible jest for life had filled his body with unprecedented energy and vigour.

Hari Dash asked in his archetypal, apprehensive voice: "If the snakes come down from the tree and bite us?"

Dasa Pradhan kept staring at the flood water constantly and said: "In this flood, the enemies and friends are all alike. There were a black cobra and a boa taking shelter on the same floating roof on which we also had taken shelter." Hari Dash still could not be convinced and asked in a petrified voice: "If the rising water submerges this isle and if the snakes come down?"

Jayee Mohanty answered in a taunting voice: "Hey Hari Dash! You are a lone person. If you die, there is nobody behind you to even shed a single drop of tear on your derelict, abandoned corpse. Why are you so possessive and finicky about your sordid, solitary and companionless life?" There was a note of scathing sarcasm in his voice that penetrated into the depths of Hari Dash's slender bones like a cold, biting, wintry shiver. Hari Dash played harmonium in the village theatre group; he was its music teacher. He was so indulged in that group's musical activities that he couldn't find some convenient time for marriage and thus, remained single all through.

Hari Dash kept troubling everybody with his nagging, irksome and unfounded fear. But Jayee Mohanty's taunt seriously disturbed his mind, like an oceanic convulsion. Who was after him, truly? He was almost forty. He couldn't get married till now. His age was also passing and he was getting older day by day. If he was swept away in the flood, the village folks won't even bother to search for his body. Then why should he bother so much for a life that had become uneventful, derelict and barren? But his desire for living was incredibly insistent and irrepressible. After all, man cannot relinquish his desire to live even in the midst of the acutest hazards and adversities.

Hari Dash went to a safe distance from the tree and tried to measure the water level. The radio announcement was right; the water shall rise. By this time, the level had already risen by a few inches more.

Dasa Pradhan said: "Today is the thirteenth day."

Hari Dash asked in a perturbed voice: "So what?"

"It's the full moon night and the moon's gravitational pull is in full swing. The billowing water-logging does not get cleared therefore. The swelling and surging tide doesn't allow the influx of river water into the sea. That means the flood water shall rise further." Explained Dasa Pradhan.

A helicopter was found flying very low while relentlessly rambling in the air, circuitously. Hari Dash lifted his hands and shouted: "Hey! Save us."

Phagu Rout said: "Hey! Hey! Have you gone mad? Shall the helicopter save us?"

Hari Dash said: "Then why it is flying in the air?"

Phagu Rout answered in a tone imbued with covetous sarcasm: "The sagacious ministers are greeting you from above, with benevolence and devotion. This is a clear and irrefutable testimony to their service to the people, to their never-ending humanitarian enterprise. The newspaper and the radio shall inundate them with boundless accolades and admirations."

Dasa Pradhan listened to all these while chewing a shrivelled piece of grass. He responded: "In earlier times, these ministers came on banana-trunk-made boats risking their lives."

Phagu Rout answered: "You don't understand. Today is the age of technology. Now the flood relief missions are carried out in a scientific manner; even though the flood is man-made, artificial. The time you speak of was different. Flood occurred when Lord Indra poured heavy rainfall on Earth, with divine wrath and vengeance against mankind's outrageous violations of 'dharma.' Now the engineers generate flood by opening the gates of the huge water-reservoirs."

Two more helicopters came rambling through the sky like two giant vultures with hitched, metallic wings.

Hari Dash lifted his hands into the air and shouted: "Hey Helicopters! Save us. Save us."

The food-packets thrown from the helicopters floated on the water surface, like rotten clusters of jasmines. Hari Dash asked: "What are these packets?"

Phagu Pradhan answered: "These are food packets. Have you not heard of food packets being distributed from helicopters during flood?"

Dasa Pradhan said: "They are distributing the food packets to the fishes. Will they ever reach the people caught up in the circumambient water-logging?"

Now they realized they have not eaten anything since yesterday. Their stomachs burnt in oppressive hunger that ran amok through their emptied stomachs like a congregated cluster of a hundred, squeaking mice. The scorching sun was hovering overhead like a revolving fireball emitting blazing rays of fire. Three or four paper-enwrapped food packets fell a few meters away from the Talabani isle. One of them fell within the diameters of Govinda Pattanaik's reach.

Somebody said: "Hey Pattanaik! Lift those packets before they are swept away in the turbulent stream." Pattanaik stretched his hand to catch hold of the packets. But for some strange and inexplicable reason, he drew them back allowing the food packets to drift away, in clumsy and disjointed clusters."

Dasa Pradhan asked in a stupefied voice: "What happened?" Alas! It would have been better if he caught hold of those packets. They had not eaten anything for three days. There was not a single morsel of food left in their stomachs.

Govind Pattanaik said: "I won't eat food thrown at us as if thrown at beggars. In the last flood also, we had not eaten food for three consecutive days. After three days, a few people came on a banana-trunk-made boat and offered us parched rice and jaggery."

"Then was it not begged food?" Asked Phagu Pradhan in a bantering voice.

Govind Pattanaik answered: "No! No! They had offered us food with grace and honour. There was an ingrained sense of respect and dignity in that offer. It was not like throwing food from the sky and taking undue credit."

Phagu Pradhan stopped arguing and kept mum for he knew that it was fruitless in engaging in an argument with these abstruse, unyielding and rigid-minded older generation people. They had their own stupid and bizarre ways of understanding things and they could not be easily convinced about novel ideas and new ways of living. They were not ready to digest that their generation is outdated.

Jayee Mohanty shouted at somebody, in a shrilling voice: "Hey! You will drown. You will be swept with the current." Nata Kandi had entered deep into chest-high water to drag a few food packets floating away from him on undulating water. Holding three/four food packets in his hand, he came out.

Phagu Rout shouted in a tone of utter desperation: "Hey! Give one to me! Give one to me!" Nata threw one packet at him, unhesitatingly.

Jati Nanda was the revered village priest. His gluttonous mouth started watering looking at the food packets in a scenario where extreme hunger had made his stomach shrink without food. But how could he accept food from a barber? His sacred thread would be polluted and it would be a horrendous act of sacrilege for a sanctimonious priest like him whose consecrated body, mind and spirit were united in a hallowed, divine conjugation. He would have to undergo stringent purification rites, if he collected the food packet, unscrupulously, from a low-caste barber by transgressing the proscriptions of his 'dharma' and thereby, defiling its protected sanctity. Despite all his sacred inhibitions, he still could not control his curiosity and asked in a seemingly indifferent voice: "What food is there inside, boy?"

Nata Kandi opened one packet. There were two pieces of bread, some jaggery, two boiled potatoes, one candle light and a match box. Nata Kandi said to himself: "I wish they kept a few 'bidi's there."

Jati Nanda kept looking at the opened-up packet, surreptitiously, while trying to evade the hawk-eyed glare of the congregated and starving villagers. His stomach burnt in unbearable hunger. He saw Nata engulf the breads and jaggery at one go and looking at that scene, the abrupt and inextinguishable fire of hunger started burning more vigorously inside his starving belly. But he was helplessly caught in the whirlpool of a moral dilemma, an ethical imbroglio—how to collect food from an abominable low-caste wretch? But then, then suddenly an old saying from ancient scriptures flashed across the dark space of his mind like a sudden, evanescent meteor and readily resolved his moral dilemma. The saying was: "In utter need, there is no law" and its corollary was that everybody is the same when it comes to the question of hunger. With all his ethical dilemmas resolved thus, Jati Nanda said: "Hey Nata! Has the government thrown the packet only for you?" Jayee Mohanty is and old and ailing man. Why don't you give a packet to him?"

Nata was busy engulfing one boiled potato while peeling another's skin. He answered in an irritated voice:

"When did I say no?" And then he started moving towards Jayee Mohanty to give him one packet."

Jayee Mohanty said: "Hey! Hey! Did you not understand Nata? Give that packet to Jati Nana[54]."

Jati Nanda almost confiscated that packet from Nata's hand and shouted vociferously such that everybody could listen: "In utter need, there is no law." Then he tore one packet with an expressive show of frenetic desperation and hurriedly gobbled one piece of bread. While chewing it with a crackling sound, he said: "Hey! Eating this bread is like chewing leather." Saying this, he bit his tongue apologetically. How could he utter such putrid words, being a devout Brahmin? Chewing leather . . .?

Phagu Rout got up from his place and ran berserk towards the isle's western side that had moved into deeper waters like an elongated peninsula.

Nata asked him: "Hey Phagu Babu! Why did you run there so frantically as if being entranced by a ghost?" Hari also came rushing in, fearing the unpropitious advent of a new danger.

Nata Kandi shouted while pointing his trembling finger at some hazy and unclear thing floating on water: "Mother Ganga! Mother Ganga!" Then everybody, keened by his voluble scream, looked in that direction curiously, including Dasa Pradhana. After casually surveying the scene, he sat down, with a condescending and disinterested disposition that was emphatically succinct on his face. Govind Pattanaik did not get up from his seat at all, and said: "A destitute lady comes floating on a roof."

---

54   A Brahmin priest is called 'Nana' in colloquial language.

In fact, they had also come floating on a roof like this once in another flood.

Nata Kandi started screaming again in another high-pitched voice: "Glory to Mother Ganga! Glory to Mother Ganga."

Nobody could conjecture from which flood-inundated village this blown-away roof came floating? One curly and twisted pumpkin creeper was still stuck curvaceously on its thatched top. A tiny and fresh flower had bloomed incandescently in that creeper; it kept tossing its flippant head to and fro in the whirly and rain-splattered moist wind, heedless of the utter devastation reigning all around. The lady sat on the roof like the sedentary effigy of an unknown goddess; she had dishevelled hair; her tell-tale dark and provocative eyes looked wide, stimulating and fluorescent; the eyeballs remained stubbornly insensate and unmoved and their adamantine immovability could be spotted from a distance. A faint and half-erased, rubicund vermilion mark still glimmered on her head, unwittingly, like the fractured and dispossessed fragment of a vanished star. The roof came nearer. Her face was burning bright with slanted sunrays, brushing across her rain-water-soaked, swollen face, tangentially.

Nata Kandi shouted again, this time with folded hands: "Glory to Mother Ganga! Glory to Mother Ganga."

Dasa Pradhan nevertheless spotted something worrying and comminatory and shouted with sharp-toned note of concern: "Hey! The destitute lady is floating away. Drag that roof to the shore. If the roof is captured in the whirlwind, she will drown and die."

The roof was rapidly and unwaveringly drifting

towards that murderous whirlwind. On it was sitting the destitute lady, with a grave and undeterred expression of stoic indifference dazzlingly implanted on her face, as a marker of cold and helpless acceptance of Nature's cruel and nonchalant vicissitude. She had turned speechless.

But if she was not Mother Ganga incarnate, would she not have shouted: 'Save me! Save me!"

Nobody dared to get into the drifting water full of swift and turbulently gyrating, murderous undercurrents. Somebody said: "Don't you all see there is not even a single blink in her eyes?"

Jati Nanda said: "Don't you all know the eyes of gods and goddesses never blink?"

Dasa Pradhan shouted: "Hey men! Get into the water. Get into the water and save the lady. She is floating away. I presume all her family members have been swept away by the flood's alacritous, pillaging, and drifty currents. She is perhaps the lone survivor. She has become deaf and dumb out of insurmountable grief and terror that have seized her after her interminable sense of loss. It happens like this with a traumatized flood-survivor."

By that time Hari Dash had entered into chest-deep water and was dragging that dilapidated roof ashore.

"Get down from that roof to safety, mother! Where is your village?" Dasa Pradhan asked the lady in a softened and fatherly, affectionate voice.

The destitute lady neither got down from the roof nor responded to his soothing words, while sitting mum and decidedly unresponsive towards the gratuitous bunch of gathered people looking at her with expressive airs of keenness and concern. She kept staring at them, dumbfounded, while being overawed by the brooding immensity of tranquillity and weirdness of this estranged isle.

Dasa Pradhan held the lady's hand softly in his and dragged her onto the shore, to safety. The moment she landed on the isle, she burst into tears—streaming, unstoppable tears . . . There was no stopping to that piteous and heartrending wailing.

Dasa Pradhan said: "Leave her alone in that state. I am sure she has lost everybody of her family. Let her cry. Let her grievous emotions flow away through her therapeutic and relief-providing tears; let her be purged of her excruciatingly painful and agonizing emotions. Then only she will come back to her senses. Leave her alone."

The lady kept on bewailing ad nauseam and collapsed on the ground like a felled tree; her teeth were jabbed into each other; her soft hands had stiffened with the mulish and pertinacious tenacity of unbreakable metals; she had fainted. Hari Dash inserted his finger into her mouth and said: "Her teeth have been locked." And then he said worriedly: "What will happen now?"

Dasa Pradhana usually did not get provoked and irritated by anything due to his usually calm and imperturbable temperament. But Hari Dash had been constantly irritating everybody with his stupid and puerile questions. The former's patience came to end and he said in a fractious voice: "What else will happen? You are a bachelor. She has nobody with her now. So, now you will marry her and then, both will live together ever after. What else?"

Everybody started laughing boisterously.

The flood was receding. At places the sand patches were laid bare like the hard and glistening backs of tortoises slouching sluggishly across a waterless seashore's interminable stretches of sand. The massive, ripened stalks of corns were all swept away like lost, forlorn memories. The bamboo jungle of Nachhipur village started showing its drenched face from amidst the dull and insidious flood-ravaged vacuum created on the landscape by the receded waters. And also were seen from amidst the desultory masses of salvaged ruins, the broken relics of the village's dilapidated earthen houses . . . There was no trace of the Harizan[55] slum, though. There were no more food packets falling from the helicopters. The flood had subsided completely. The triumphant, cacophonic voices of ministers boasting and bolstering about their services done to humanity during the calamitous times of the flood were ceaselessly heard on Phagu Rout's transistor.

Nata Kandi said: "Let's all go back to our village. The flood water has almost receded. While going back, we might encounter occasional encumbrances formed by knee-deep or at best, waist-deep water-patches at places. But even in that case, why should we continue staying here, in this god-forsaken, marooned island, anymore with hungry stomachs, grieving hearts and tormented minds? The relief centre might have already opened in the village.

Nata Kandi was the first one to start walking, absentmindedly. Jati Nanda followed him, like his ubiquitous, uncomplaining, and obedient shadow. Dasa Pradhana and Govinda Pattanaik also started walking while muttering: "To spend time here on this swampy,

---

55   People belonging to the backward castes.

abandoned and ghostly isle with hungry stomachs was perhaps cold-heartedly scribbled in our destiny, by God Almighty."

Phagu Rout said: "Hey Jayee uncle! Get up. I will hold you by your slacked arm in my hand arm so that you walk straight, without falling. Keep walking with me." Jayee Mohanty tried to get up from the ground with his bamboo crutch. Then he asked: "Where is Hari Dash?"

Hari Dash kept watching the destitute lady, unwaveringly, under the flood-ravaged, ramshackle, spooky and battered roof. She was getting back to her senses intermittently, looking around with wide, transfixed eyes as if her eyeballs would bulge out into the air and then, fainting while bewailing inconsolably.

Hari Dash said: "I cannot go leaving her alone, in this plight."

Jayee Mohanty said in a sardonic voice: "This Hari Dash has lived all alone throughout his life. Mother Ganga has arranged a bride for her."

While holding Phagu's hand, Jayee Mohanty started walking—unsteady and tottering-- down the gravely, pebbly and winding path descending down the Talabani isle like a curvy rope, and mingling with the plain landscape lying stretched at the below like an unfurled, greenish carpet. A sarcastic smile hung on Jayee Mohanty's pale, blackish, gangrene-infested lips.

Jayee Mohanty's words ignited Hari Dash's hidden desire and his subdued prurience along with an abrupt influx of infectious desire running amok across his throbbing veins like a rapidly traversing wave. The lady lay flat on the ground, with her semi-paralysed, stiffened torso laid bare like an abandoned corpse; her half-closed eyes looked inebriated with an entrancing spell of grief; she occasionally muttered indistinct and discontinuous clusters of incoherent blabberings.

One of her breasts lied thoroughly uncovered. Hari Dash covered her breast with her own cloth which was lying unkempt and thoroughly bedraggled. He had gotten bored with his dull, apathetic and monotonous existence in Nachhipur village for so many years and that too, he was never an original inhabitant of that village. At times, a well-wisher asked: "Hari Dash! Will you never start a family?" He would mutter: "Who will give his daughter to a low-earning, forty-year-old like me?" But now it seemed as if Mother Ganga had arranged this bride for him, sympathetically, out of her own sweet volition for this lonesome, penurious devotee of hers. The lady had lost her family. The flood had swept them all away. Hari Dash also had nobody of his own.

The lady suddenly got up, screeched loudly and then sat straight on the ground, like a goddess's graffiti carved on granite stone.

The reddish light of the setting sun was scattered all over her face. Her eyes were still unblinking, and transfixed.

She asked: "Where am I? Where are they all? My Kuna and Muna?

Hari Dash was a little assured by the lady's return to her senses, unexpectedly though. He anticipated that by tomorrow morning, she would be alright. He said: "Don't worry. I am here with you. You came floating on a roof that was stuck to this Talabani isle."

The lady cried loudly again and fell flat on the ground.

It had been many times since then that she has gotten up, sat straight, perpendicular to the ground, with her legs stretched like two slender stems of a tree, shouted loudly and then, fainted. Throughout the whole night, the moonlight was flooded on her half-clothed body like a soothing, pain-relieving balm laced on her wounded torso filled with innumerable scars and abrasions--unspotted and invisible though.

Till now, Hari Dash had developed some kind of tender sympathy and fellow-feeling for the destitute lady due to her pathetic and deplorable plight caused by the devastating flood. But suddenly, this flooding deluge of moonlight splattered on her body reignited his buried, entombed passions that took the form of an extreme and manifest keenness and endearing infatuation on his part towards the destitute lady. Hari Dash kept looking at her half-revealed body with unblinking eyes and waited fortuitously till she came back to her senses again.

Nobody knew the exact time in the night. Two twittering birds reeled noisily in untraceable, circuitous trajectories in the night sky above the Talabani isle. In extreme exhaustion, Hari Dash had fallen asleep on the ground. He had anticipated that the lady would return to her senses in the morning.

When Hari got up from his sleep, the whole landscape was flooded with the morning's greyish sprinkle of light leaving the darkened and begrimed Earth awash with light and brightness. The moon had waned sufficiently in the sky leaving it spotless and pervasively greyish and pestilential. But where was that lady? The cloth-bundle that she clutched tightly in her hand when she came floating was lying out there—untouched, jumbled and abandoned. But where was she?

Hari Dash came outside. But the lady was nowhere to be found. He shouted: "Hey! Where are you?" He did not even know her name. There was a cryptic and comatose silence that prevailed all around, like a bewitching spirit engulfing every little tumult that could be heard. Like a moonstruck lunatic, Hari Dash kept sprinting along the whole landscape of the Talabani isle, from this side to that side. How could that lady disappear like this, wondrously, without leaving a trace? Or was it dream, a befuddling illusion? Or Nata Kandi was right?   Was it Mother Ganga who had appeared in this destitute lady's mysterious, airy and apparitional form?

In the morning light, Hari Dash could spot her diminishing footsteps on the mud . . .

*****

Black Eagle Books

www.blackeaglebooks.org
info@blackeaglebooks.org

Black Eagle Books, an independent publisher, was founded
as a nonprofit organization in April, 2019. It is our
mission to connect and engage the Indian diaspora
and the world at large with the best of works
of world literature published on a collaborative
platform, with special emphasis on foregrounding
Contemporary Classics and New Writing.